LOST AND FOUND

"Are you Philberta?" Nate asked. She answered the description he had been given.

"This little pig went to market, this little pig stayed at home."

"Talk sense, will you?"

"This little pig had roast beef, this little pig had none."

"Cut that out. And tell me, are you Philberta or aren't you?"

"To be honest, sir, I'm not sure anymore." She laughed again, a sad sort of laugh. Then she swept a knitting needle over her head and cried, "Let's see which one of us is real!"

And with that she attacked.

WILDERNESS #57: FEAR WEAVER

David Thompson

LEISURE BOOKS NEW YORK CITY

Dedicated to Judy, Shane, Joshua and Kyndra.

A LEISURE BOOK®

September 2008

Published by

Dorchester Publishing Co., Inc.
200 Madison Avenue
New York, NY 10016

ISBN 10: 0-8439-6093-0
ISBN 13: 978-0-8439-6093-8

Visit us on the web at www.dorchesterpub.com.

WILDERNESS #57:
FEAR WEAVER

Before

The man had tears in his eyes and spittle on his chin. He ran through the woods in a wild panic, every now and then letting out a piercing shriek. He collided with a tree, but it barely slowed him. He kept glancing over his shoulder. Twice he slashed at the air with a Green River knife.

"Stay away!" he screeched. "Stay away!'

Bursting from the undergrowth into a clearing, he fell to his hands and knees, exhausted. More spittle dribbled from his lower lip into his matted beard. He mewed in fright and looked back again, and his pale face became paler.

"God no, God no, God no, God no."

Pushing to his feet, the man thrust his knife at the forest.

"Don't you dare! I won't be easy!"

The wind had died. Not so much as a leaf or pine needle stirred in the dark woods.

"I know you are there! Show yourselves!"

The man's eyes blazed with fire. His haggard features hardened. He held the knife above his head, ready to stab. "I'm waiting!"

Something moved at the edge of the clearing to his

right and the man whirled, the knife in front of him. "You won't get me! I will kill you, do you hear me?"

A horse came out of the woods and regarded the man, its ears pricked. Whinnying, it stamped a hoof.

"They are after you too?"

The man took a step, then stopped and swatted the air. He swatted it again and again, as if trying to drive off a swarm of bees. He swung and swung, only stopping when he was too weak to continue.

The horse just stood there.

"Of course," the man said. "It's not just people. They go after everything. Deer, rabbits, elk, birds, everything. Why didn't I see it sooner? How could I have been so stupid?"

The horse bobbed its head.

"It's all right." The man smiled a crooked smile. "I won't hurt you." He moved slowly toward it, the corners of his mouth twitching. "We'll get away from here. I promise to take care of you."

The horse stamped again.

"Stay calm. That's it. I'll get on you and we'll leave this terrible place. I never should have come. But how was I to know? How was anyone to know?" The man gazed at a patch of blue far above, then at the towering cliffs that reared thousands of feet on three sides of the valley. "I thought I found heaven on earth. But I unleashed demons, didn't I? From my own seed I spawned them. From my ignorance."

The man shook. His mouth still twitching, he took another step. "You and me, boy. You and me. Let's light a shuck." He chuckled, but the sound that came from his throat was like the rattle of a dry gourd.

The next instant the horse wheeled and trotted off, its brown body dappled by shadows.

"Noooooo!" The man ran after it, but only as far as the trees.

"Come back! Please come back! I can't make it afoot. Not with them everywhere. I need you!"

The thud of hooves faded. The forest was still again.

"Lord, preserve me. I'm doomed." The man raised his left hand to his brow. "I can't take this anymore. I just can't." Uttering a low sob, he turned.

Nearly invisible in the gloom, a cabin stood at the other side of the clearing. Small and sturdily built, it had a stone chimney from which curled writhing tendrils of smoke. Red curtains hung over the window like splashes of fresh blood.

The man gasped. He shuffled toward the cabin with reluctance, as if he didn't quite believe it was there, or as if the cabin nursed a new fear that made his legs weak.

"I am not, I can not, I will not," he said.

A dozen feet out the man stopped. From within came humming, low and soft and peaceful. He stood and listened for a good long while. Only when a brisk gust from off the heights fanned the nape of his neck and sent goose bumps rippling down his skin did he stir and step to the door. He didn't knock. He didn't call out and ask permission to enter. He simply worked the wooden latch and strode in.

The cabin was warm and cozy and filled with the scent of burning logs. A bearskin rug covered the middle of the floor. To the left was a log table with log benches. To the right, the doorway to a pantry. Straight ahead was the hearth. In a rocking chair beside it, calmly knitting, was a woman in an ankle-length dress and a bonnet. She hummed as her long needles clacked and clicked. When a log popped, she stared serenely at the flames.

"Jack Sprat, Jack Sprat, why do you keep doing that?"

The man coughed.

Glancing up, the woman placed her knitting in her lap. "I do declare. How long have you been there?"

"Where?" the man asked.

"Have you heard?"

"Heard what?"

"Jack Sprat could eat no fat, his wife could eat no lean. And so between the two of them, they licked the platter clean."

"I am not Jack Sprat," the man said.

The woman smiled. "Of course we are. We have always been. That was our heaven, that was our sin. But what to do now? Where to begin? I'm happy you are here. Come on in."

"I already am. Do you know where you are?"

"Don't you?" The woman heaved her bulk out of the rocking chair, grunting with the effort. "Sing a song of sixpence, a pocket full of rye. Four and twenty blackbirds, baked in a pie."

"I don't like to eat blackbird," the man said. "Too stringy and dry."

"Isn't Tommy Thumb's song pretty? That Tommy Thumb sure was witty." The woman set her knitting on the rocking chair. From a bag next to it she took another long needle and made a circle in the air. "Baa, baa, black sheep, have you any wool? Yes, sir. Yes, sir. Three bags full."

"I haven't any wool," the man said. "Only this." He wagged his knife.

"Bow, wow, wow, whose dog art thou?" the woman quoted.

"I think I am yours. Can you help me? I saw a horse, but it ran away. You can never trust horses."

The woman walked to the table and placed her hands on her stout hips. "Twinkle, twinkle, little star. How I wonder what you are." She motioned. "Come, won't you play with me?"

"It is hard," the man said.

"Try."

"Very well." The man's brow knit. "Will you take a walk with me, my little wife, today?"

The woman uttered a sharp bark of a laugh. "You can do better than that, surely. If you want my help, that is."

"I want it more than anything," the man admitted. Again his brow furrowed. "The Lord is my shepherd, I shall not want."

"Oh, come now. That is hardly in the spirit of things." The woman untied her bonnet and then tied it again. "I'm waiting. If you insist on this intrusion, you must at least be gallant."

"I never could," the man said. But his brow puckered a third time. "One, two, buckle my shoe. Three, four, knock at the door. Five, six . . ." The man stopped. "I can't remember the rest."

"You must. What do you want me to take you for? If that is your best, no wonder we are where we are."

"It always comes back to that, doesn't it?" The man paused. "Five, six, pick up sticks. Seven, eight, set them straight. Nine, ten, a big fat hen. Eleven, twelve, dig and delve."

The woman squealed in delight. "You did it! You actually and truly did it! I am very proud of you."

"Don't expect more. They made me say it day after day so I would learn my numbers. Why it has stuck with me all these years is beyond me. Our minds are a strange place."

"Birds of a feather flock together, and so do pigs and swine." The woman moved to the counter. She picked up a pan, hefted it, and set it back down. "What help can I be? I can cook and bake, I can sweep and rake."

"We must leave. Together. Now."

The woman laughed. "You jest, sir. Leave my humble home? Leave my rocking chair and my knitting? What kind of woman do you take me for? What would my husband think?"

"Don't remind me. The fog has cleared. I wish I couldn't remember, but I do."

"If wishes were horses, beggars would ride. If turnips were watches, I'd wear one at my side."

"You can stop that now."

"As I went to Bonner, I met a pig with a wig, upon my word and honor," the woman recited.

"Please stop."

"You started it," she retorted. "Then to bring them into this. To think you thought you knew it all, only to find out you knew nothing."

"Please."

"I have my moments, too, you know. I will help if you will tell me what kind of help I can be."

The man wearily stepped to the table and sat on a bench. "It's been so long. I'm no longer sure of what is and what isn't. I have to pinch myself sometimes." So saying, he pinched his cheek as hard as he could. "I think I am real."

Chuckling merrily, so that her whole body quivered like a great dish of pudding, the woman pointed a thick finger at him. "I bet I know what you would like more than anything. How empty is your belly?"

"So empty it is scraping my backbone." The man folded his arms on the table and lowered his face onto them. His next words were muffled. "They were after me a while ago. Right before I saw the horse. They might be after the horse now."

"The man in the wilderness asked me how many strawberries grew in the sea but I didn't tell him."

"God in heaven. Is this what we have come to? Is this to be our end?" The man slowly straightened. Tears were in his eyes. "Will you fill my belly or not?"

"Pat-a-cake, pat-a-cake, baker's man. Make me a cake as fast as you can. Prick it, and pat it, and mark it with a T. And put it in the oven for my Sully and me."

"Is that yes or no?"

"Little Jack Horner sat in the corner, eating his Christmas pie."

"I asked you not to do that."

The woman opened a cupboard. "What would you like? Waffles and eggs? Elk meat? Corn dodgers? How about apple dumplings? I think of all the food in the world, apple dumplings are my favorite."

The man stared at the empty shelves in the cupboard. His throat bobbed and he wiped an arm across his eyes. "How long have you been without?"

"My dears, my dears, calm your fears."

"I never would have guessed. You don't look as if you have lost weight." The man's eyes narrowed. "Wait. You *haven't* lost any. How can that be? How have you lasted?"

The woman beamed jovially and twined her fingers together. "Old Mother Hubbard went to the cupboard to get her poor doggie a bone. But when she got there the cupboard was bare, so the poor doggie got none."

"One more and I will scream. I swear to God I will."

"There was an old woman who lived in a shoe. She had so many children she didn't know what to do."

The man was off the bench and reached her in three bounds. Gripping her by the arms, he shook her as hard as he could.

"Stop it! Stop it! Stop it!"

The woman went on beaming. "Calm yourself, Sully. Haven't I always taken care of you?" She cupped his chin and gazed deep into his eyes. "My sweet, sour, splendid, awful, caring, cold codpiece."

Sully staggered back, his cheeks damp. He groped behind him until his hand found the rough-hewn table. Sinking onto the bench, he trembled. "I can feel it clawing at me. It never stops. When it takes hold I am lost to everything. But then I come out of it for a while, like you."

"Bat, bat, come under my hat, and I'll give you a slice of bacon." The woman chortled. "Is that what you would like to eat? A bat?"

"Philberta, please. I did all I could. I'm sorry it wasn't enough. The thing now is to get away. We must leave while I am clear in the head. Try to shake it off so we—" Sully stopped at a sudden scratching at the door, as if a claw was scraping it from top to bottom. "No. Not now."

"My darlings!" Philberta happily exclaimed. "They have come to pay me another visit. I wonder what sweetmeats they have brought me this time." She started toward the door, but Sully got there ahead of her and thrust out his hand.

"No! Think! You know what is out there. You know what they will do to us."

As if to prove him right, from the other side of the

door came a low growl, followed by more, and harder, scratching.

"Let me past," Philberta insisted, and shoved him out of her way. "Rub-a-dub-dub, three men in a tub. And who do you think they be?" She placed her hand on the latch.

Sully shoved her and she stumbled back. "I will not warn you again! Heed me, woman!"

"Heed a fool? What would that make me? Twice the idiot?" Philberta shook her head. "You have come to the wrong place if it is heeding you are after."

The scratching became a frenzy of clawing and growls and snarls. The door shook to fierce blows, the leather hinges creaking.

"Do you hear them?" Philberta asked. "Aren't they grand?"

Sully faced the door and raised his knife. "I am ready for them! If they get in, there will be the devil to pay."

Philberta stepped to the counter and gripped a cast iron pan. "Dickery, dickery dare, the pig flew up in the air." She walked up behind Sully and brought the pan crashing down on the top of his head. The *crunch* of his skull was loud and final. He slumped onto his side, briefly convulsed, and went limp.

"Serves him right," Philberta said. Fluffing her hair, she called out, "Can you hear me, my sweets?"

Something outside the door howled.

"Birds of a feather flock together," Philberta said, and opened it.

Godsend

Few natural wonders stirred Nate King like the Rocky Mountains. He still remembered the first time he set eyes on them: the emerald foothills, the green of the thick timber that covered the higher slopes, the brown of the rocky heights crowned by white caps of snow. Peaks that reared miles into the sky. Compared to the splendor of the Rockies, the mountains of his native New York were so many pitiful bumps.

On this particular morning Nate was many miles from the remote valley his family called home. He was astride his favorite bay, on his way to the village of his wife's cousin, Touch The Clouds. The Shoshones were contemplating a raid on their enemies the Blackfeet, and Touch The Clouds wanted Nate to sit in on the council. It showed the high regard in which the Shoshones held him. That, and Nate suspected the Shoshones hoped he would help them get their hands on a few more rifles.

The last thing Nate expected to come across so deep in the mountains were other whites. But from high atop a ridge Nate spied eight riders, the last leading a couple of pack horses, winding west in his direction. They had no inkling he was there.

Nate was heading north. He raised his reins to ride on, but curiosity got the better of him. Reaching back, he opened a beaded parfleche his wife had made and brought out a collapsible metal tube. Extending it, he pressed the scalloped eyepiece to his eye.

Nate was a big man, broad of shoulder and narrow of waist. He was dressed in buckskins. A beaver hat crowned his black thatch of hair. An ammo pouch, powder horn and possibles bag crisscrossed his broad chest. Wedged under his wide leather belt were a pair of flintlocks, while jutting from a beaded saddle sheath was the stock of a Hawken rifle. On his right hip hung a bowie, on his left a tomahawk. He was, in short, a walking arsenal. He needed to be.

As Nate studied the eight riders through his spyglass, his mouth curled in a frown. "I'll be switched," he said to his bay. Four of the eight in particular were responsible for his frown. "Some folks have no more sense than a tree stump."

Angry, Nate snapped the telescope in upon itself, and shoved it into his parfleche. "They are none of my business," he declared, and again went to ride on to the north and the Shoshone village.

Nate hesitated. His conscience pricked him, as it often did in situations like this. For long minutes he debated whether to go on or go down and talk to the party below. Exasperated with himself, he reined sharply down the slope.

The lead rider spotted him and pointed. As well the man should, since he, like Nate, was a frontiersman.

Nate threaded through a belt of lodgepole pines and came out on a flat bench. Rather than go lower, he drew rein and dismounted to await the eight. It was a quarter of an hour before they reached him, and in that time Nate gathered dead limbs, used his fire steel and flint, and tinder from his tinderbox, to kindle a fire, and put coffee on to brew.

When the other frontiersman came over the crest, Nate was seated on a log he had dragged close to the fire, his Hawken across his legs. He didn't smile or lift a hand in greeting. Instead, he leveled the Hawken and said bluntly, "I should kill you here and now."

The man made no attempt to raise his own rifle. Lean and bony, he had a high forehead, stringy brown hair that hung limp under a floppy brown hat, and a jagged scar where his left ear should be. "I thought it might be you. Not many are your size."

"My son tells me you were there when he was whipped." Nate was referring to an incident not long ago in which his oldest, Zach, had tangled with an English lord.

"Did he also tell you I had no hand in the whipping? And that I did what I could to help him escape?"

Nate slowly lowered the Hawken. The mere thought of harm coming to either of his children was enough to fill him with fury. He loved Zach and Evelyn dearly and devotedly, and anyone who hurt them must answer to him. "He told me, Ryker. Which is why I'm not going to blow out your wick."

Edwin Ryker let out a long breath. "You had me worried there. I don't want you for an enemy."

"We have never been bosom friends."

The other riders were filing onto the bench. A white-haired bantam of a woman in a floral dress and yellow bonnet jabbed a bony finger at Nate and demanded, "Why were you pointing your rifle at our guide just now? If you are a brigand, all you will get from us is an early grave."

"Aunt Aggie, please," said a man of fifty or so. His clothes were store bought. He had a thin mustache and thin sideburns and no chin to speak off. "Hush, and let us men handle this."

The woman who had threatened Nate was not the least bit intimidated. "Pshaw, Peter. Men are good for two things in this world. As beasts of burden and to help breed. Beyond that, we women would be better off without you."

Nate laughed.

Aunt Aggie's back became ramrod straight. "Find me humorous, do you, you great lump of muscle?"

"I find you marvelous. My wife would agree with your opinion of my gender. She has tongue-lashed my ears many a time."

"I dare say you deserved it," Aunt Aggie said, but she was smiling. "Although I must admire her taste. For a lump of muscle you are uncommonly handsome."

A woman about the same age as Peter let out with a loud sigh. "Enough, Aggie. Must you always embarrass us?"

"I speak my mind, Erleen. You would do well to do the same. Timidity never got anyone anywhere."

"We don't know this man from Adam, yet you carry on with him like some tavern tart. I wish just once you would remember you are supposed to act like a lady. And if you can't do that, at least act your age."

"Did you hear her?" Aunt Aggie said to Nate. "She was born with a sour disposition, and life has not improved it much."

"Agatha!" Erleen declared. "I will thank you to

shush until we find out who this man is and whether he is trustworthy."

"I can answer both questions," Edwin Ryker said. "This here is Nate King. He got his start as a free trapper years ago, and now he lives somewhere in these mountains with his family and a few close friends. As for trusting him, he is as trustworthy as a man can be this side of walking on water."

"That is some recommendation," Aunt Aggie said.

Peter kneed his horse forward, dismounted, and held out a hand as limp as his hair. "Permit me to introduce us. I am Peter Woodrow out of Philadelphia, Pennsylvania."

Nate wondered if they were Quakers, but then quickly realized they must not be since they were armed. Quakers never, ever carried guns; they didn't believe in violence of any kind.

"This fine woman is my wife, Erleen. Agatha is her older sister. All of us call her Aunt Aggie. We've hired Mr. Ryker on an urgent matter and have spent the better part of two weeks making our way ever deeper into these mountains."

The last four riders had come over the top. It confirmed what Nate had seen through his spyglass, and his frown returned. Standing, he rounded on Edwin Ryker. "What in God's name are you doing, bringing these pilgrims this far in? Have you warned them they could lose their hair?"

"Many a time and then some," Ryker replied. "Don't be mad at me. They would have come by themselves if they couldn't find a guide. The way I look at it, I'm doing them a favor. And being paid for it."

"You seem agitated, Mr. King," Aunt Aggie said.

"I have reason to be. You folks are asking for grief. You've made a mistake. You shouldn't be here."

"Care to tell us why?" Peter asked.

"Where to begin?" Nate scratched his chin. "Let's start with the meat-eaters. Most haven't been killed off, as they have east of the Mississippi. They are everywhere. Then there are the hostiles. Indians who will slit your throat for no other reason than you are white. And even if you are lucky and don't run into a griz or a war party, your horse could throw you and you could break a leg or come down sick. And there aren't any doctors."

"That was some speech, handsome."

"Aggie, please," Erleen said, and turned to Nate. "We appreciate your concern, Mr. King. But you are the one who is mistaken. We *must* be here, come what may."

Peter nodded. "We are looking for someone."

"And did you have to bring *them*?" Nate asked, nodding at the last four riders. More of the Woodrow brood: two boys and two girls, all smartly dressed.

"Of course," Peter said. "We are a family. We do everything together. Where Erleen and I go, our children go." He pointed at a spitting image of himself. "That's Fitch. He is eighteen." He pointed at his other son, who took after the mother. "That's Harper. He's seventeen. As you can see, both are armed, and fair shots."

"Fair isn't always good enough out here."

Peter Woodrow pointed at a girl in a blue bonnet. "That's Anora. She's fifteen, and as fine a little lady as a father could ask for."

"Pleased to meet you, sir."

Peter indicated the last of his offspring. "And this is Tyne, our youngest. She's only twelve, and a lively bundle, if I do say so myself."

Tyne smiled sweetly. Unlike the rest of her family,

who all had dark eyes and dark hair, Tyne had straw-colored curls, and her eyes were lake blue, like Nate's own. "Aren't these mountains wonderful, Mr. King?"

"They can be deadly, too."

"As Aunt Aggie likes to say, we can't fret over what might never happen. She says we should look for the good in life, not the bad."

Agatha grinned. "I am a regular sage."

"I wish I could make you understand," Nate said.

"We have done well so far," Peter said. "The dangers in these mountains have been exaggerated."

"That they have," Erleen agreed. "To hear folks back home talk, we should have been scalped the minute we crossed the Mississippi River."

Nate sighed. "You mentioned that you are searching for someone?"

"My younger brother, Sullivan," Peter answered. "He came west with his wife and three boys about a year and a half ago. He managed to get a letter back to us shortly after they got here, and then nothing. I mean to find out if he is still alive, and if not, to learn his fate."

"He came to the Rockies?" Nate was mildly surprised. He could count the number of settlers on two hands and have fingers left over. "I've never heard of any Sullivan Woodrow."

Peter gestured at the towering peaks to the west. "Sully is somewhere in there. He wrote us how to find his cabin. Even with his directions, though, Mr. Ryker is having a hard time."

Edwin Ryker had been listening to their exchange. Now he addressed Nate, saying, "I've read the letter. You won't believe it. This Sully wanted to live as a trapper."

"The beaver trade died out long ago."

"You know that and I know that, but this Sully figured there must be enough beaver and other animals around to make a living."

Nate grunted. A man *could* make a living at it. Good furs were always in demand. But trapping was hard, brutal work, and the money to be made wasn't enough for a family of five to live comfortably. "Was this Sully a woodsman? Could he live off the land?"

"I would rather you didn't use the past tense," Peter said. "And yes, my brother is the best woodsman I know. Back East, he spent nearly all his time hunting or fishing. One year he brought down six deer."

"Sully has always loved the outdoors," Erleen added. "The forest was in his blood."

Nate wasn't impressed. The wilds of the East were nothing like the wilds of the West. It could well be that Sully had no idea what he was letting himself in for when he brought his family to the Rockies. "What was this about directions?"

It was Ryker who answered. "The letter mentions a few landmarks. If I've read it right, Sullivan's cabin is on the other side of this range."

"Over the divide?"

Ryker nodded. "In a high valley. He mentions sandstone cliffs that can be seen for miles. One is split down the middle and looks like a giant *V*."

Nate gave a slight start.

"What? Do you know where the valley is?"

"I might." Nate had wandered all over the central Rockies when he was a trapper. From the geyser country to the deserts of the Southwest, he knew the land well.

Erleen Woodrow clasped her hands. "That's wonderful news! You are a godsend, Mr. King."

"How so?"

"You can take us there. It would save us considerable time, and we would be ever so grateful."

"I'd be in your debt," Peter stressed.

Nate stared at the stark heights they were making for. "If I'm right, your brother picked country few whites have ever set foot in."

"The very kind Sully wanted."

"Bears and the like will be as thick as fleas on an old hound. And there are bound to be Indians."

"Is that a yes or a no?" Aunt Aggie asked.

Nate stared at her, then at the two sons and the girls. His gaze lingered on young Tyne's innocent features. He thought of his own daughter, Evelyn, and he gave the only answer he could.

Into the Heart of Darkness

Late summer in the Rockies.

The lush green of a wet spring had given way to the parched greens and somber shades of dry day after dry day. At the lower elevations withering heat blistered man and beast. But up in the high country, while it was every bit as dry, it wasn't quite as hot.

As best Nate could judge, the pass he and the others were making for was at ten thousand feet. He had been over it only once, many summers ago when he and hundreds of other trappers were prowling in search of streams and rivers that might harbor the industrious creatures their livelihoods depended on.

At this altitude the air had a rarified quality that made Nate conscious of each breath he took. His lungs had to work a little harder; he had to breathe a little deeper.

The timberline was below them. Above were a series of steep slopes littered with treacherous talus and dotted with boulders. The ping of metal horseshoes on rock was constant as their animals strained to defy the cant, and gravity.

Nate was in the lead. They had been climbing for

hours when he came to a shelf and drew rein to await the rest.

Edwin Ryker was close behind. He swung his sorrel in next to Nate's bay and idly scratched the scar where his left ear had been. "We need to talk."

"Flap your gums but keep it short." Nate was keeping an eye on Erleen Woodrow. Her mare was giving her trouble. It didn't help that Erleen wasn't much of a rider.

"What do you expect to get out of this? They are paying me a hundred dollars, and I'll be damned if I will share."

"Did I ask you to?"

"Not yet."

Nate shifted his gaze from the struggling mare to Ryker. "I have no interest in their money."

"Then why put your life in danger for a bunch of strangers?"

"They need help."

"That's it?" Ryker snorted. "I never took you for the noble type. Your son certainly isn't."

Nate placed his hand on one of the .55-caliber flintlocks tucked under his leather belt. "Insult me or my son again and you will find out exactly how noble I'm not."

"Sheath your claws," Ryker said quickly. "I have nothing against you. But we're different, you and me. I'd never help these yacks if they weren't paying me. They are sheep waiting to be slaughtered."

"You don't care about anyone but yourself, is that how it goes?"

"I make no bones about how I am."

"Says the man who helped my son escape from men who were out to kill him. You are not the ogre you would like us to believe."

Ryker laughed. "I don't give a good damn what anyone thinks. As for your son, I helped him to spare my hide. There was a chance he might have gotten away on his own and come after me later. I didn't want that. Your boy is a holy terror when he is out for blood."

Nate opened his mouth to dispute it but didn't. Ryker was right. Zach *was* a terror when his blood-lust was up, so much so, Nate often worried about what the future held for his hot-tempered pride and joy.

"So tell me. Are you thinking what I am thinking about Sullivan and his family?" Ryker asked.

"There's a chance they are still alive."

"You know better. It has been more than a year since anyone heard from them. We'll find bones if we find anything, and then only if we find the valley and their cabin."

"Do you always look at the bright side?"

Ryker laughed again. "I like you, King. For a mountain man you would make a fine schoolmarm."

The mare was floundering. Stones and dirt cascaded from under her scrabbling hooves as she sought to keep her balance. Erleen leaned well back, the reins taut in her white-knuckled hands.

Cupping a hand to his mouth, Nate hollered, "Bend forward, over the saddle!"

"See what I mean about yacks?" Ryker said. "These infants don't even know how to ride."

"Bend forward!" Nate shouted again, and this time the woman listened. Almost immediately, the mare regained its footing and laboriously climbed the final twenty feet to the shelf.

"Praise God!" Erleen exclaimed. "I thought for sure I would take an awful fall."

Ryker winked at Nate. "See what I've had to put up with?"

"How much farther to the pass?" Erleen asked.

"Another hour yet." Nate checked the rest, but no one else was in trouble. Peter was a fair rider. The four youngsters did better than their parents, but none of them could compare to Aunt Aggie, who controlled her mount with superb skill. "That sister of yours can handle herself."

"Agatha? Well, she is older than me by almost twenty years." Erleen fiddled with her bonnet. "Our folks had nine children. She was the eldest, and I was the youngest."

Ryker said, "One kid would be one too many for me. Brats at ten are brats at twenty, and I can do without the aggravation."

"Must you be so crude, Mr. Ryker? I have asked you before to be civil, and it would delight me greatly if you would at least try."

"What are you in a huff about? All I said was that most kids are brats."

Peter joined them, then the girls, then Fitch and Harper. Last to reach safety was Aunt Aggie. Her cheeks were flushed and her eyes were twinkling with excitement. She brightened even more when Nate complimented her riding.

"Thank you, kind sir. It is unfortunate you have a wife. My third husband died on me five years ago and I have not come across a likely replacement."

Erleen colored from neckline to hairline. "Is there no end? Have you no modesty or decorum? And in front of Anora and Tyne, no less."

"That's all right, Mother," Anora said. "We don't mind. We like Aunt Aggie."

"She is the best aunt ever," Tyne agreed.

"Agatha can be charming, I grant you," Erleen responded. "But she can also be as crude as Mr. Ryker, and I would rather she doesn't influence you with her sinful ways."

"Oh Lord," Aunt Aggie said.

"Don't take that tone with me, sister. Three husbands is two too many. You always have been too lax when it comes to men and your tart tongue."

"I should hope so," Aunt Aggie said.

Since Peter was imitating a lump of clay, Nate held up a hand. "Enough, ladies. I don't care to listen to you bicker every foot of the way."

"Oh, this is normal for us," Aunt Aggie said. "My little sister has always thought she is better than I. She never passes up an opportunity to point out my flaws."

"You are impossible," Erleen said.

Peter finally stirred. "You heard Mr. King."

Nate reined the bay around. Other than pockets of scrub brush and a few small boulders, the next slope presented no problems. He twisted to mention to the others to be sure to string out in single file, and happened to glance past them at the forest below.

It took a few seconds for Nate to realize what he was seeing. Then he blinked and it was gone.

Ryker was next to him, and asked, "What was that look on your face just now?"

"Have you seen sign of anyone following you since you hooked up with the Woodrows?"

"No. Why do you ask?" Ryker twisted to scan the lower slopes. "Is someone trailing us?"

"At least one."

"White or red?"

"He was too far off, and in the shadows."

"So it could be either." Ryker scowled. "Damn. And here I thought I was doing a good job of keeping them safe."

"I thought you didn't care about anything except the money."

"They can all be scalped for all I care," Ryker snapped. "I'm only thinking of my reputation. People aren't going to want to hire me for a guide if I go and get some of them killed."

"Be careful, Edwin."

"Huh?"

"I'm beginning to like you."

"Go to hell." Ryker jabbed his heels and rode on.

Chuckling, Nate stayed where he was and motioned for the rest to go on by him. Peter nodded as he went past. Erleen smiled. Aunt Aggie drew rein.

"Resting so soon? I figured someone with as many muscles as you must have stamina to spare."

"It's a good thing my wife isn't here. She would shoot you."

Aunt Aggie grinned in delight, then sobered. "Be honest with me. I saw you whispering with Smelly. What is going on?"

"Smelly?"

"My nickname for our guide. Haven't you noticed? If you are near him when the wind is right, you would swear you were downwind of a barrel of rotten apples. And that is being charitable."

It was Nate's turn to grin. "Baths aren't considered a necessity out here."

"You must be a reader," Aunt Aggie said. "I can always tell by the words people use. And only a reader uses 'necessity.' Smelly would have said something like, 'Baths ain't good for you,' and then scratched his armpit and smelled his fingers."

Despite his concern, Nate indulged in a belly laugh. "I do happen to own a couple dozen books. I have my mother to thank. She loved to read. She turned me into a reader when I was six and I have been reading ever since."

"Smart woman. But then readers always are. Our brains need fertilizer just like plants or they go to weed like Smelly's."

A cough came from behind her. The four offspring had drawn rein and were waiting for her to go on.

"Our folks are getting too far ahead," Fitch said.

"We will talk books later," Aunt Aggie told Nate, and clucked to her horse.

Fitch and Harper rode past. Anora remarked that she was sore from all the riding. Tyne came to a stop and fixed those trusting blue eyes of hers on Nate.

"Why are Indians following us, Mr. King?"

Nate almost swore. "You've seen some?"

"Oh, yes. There are four of them. They are being sneaky, but I spotted them when I was swatting at a fly that wouldn't leave me alone. I didn't let on that I knew they were back there." Tyne chortled. "They are funny, the way they go from tree to tree and try to stay hid."

"Why didn't you let me know?"

"I'm sorry. Should I have? No one told me. Mother said that if any Indians came up to me I was to smile and be friendly so they would be nice, but those Indians haven't come close yet." Tyne fluffed at her golden curls. "They must be friendly or they would have tried to hurt us by now. And here I'd heard the most awful things about Indians."

Nate remembered a Mexican freighter he came across once down near Santa Fe. The Apaches had tied the man upside down to a wagon wheel and lit a

fire under his head. Then there were the three Con-
estogas caught unawares by Comanches. He could
think of plenty more, but he preferred not to. "From
here on out, little one, you tell me when you spot an
Indian. Anytime, day or night, whether I am awake
or asleep."

"I will." Tyne smiled and slapped her legs against
her pinto. "I better catch up. Father gets annoyed if
we fall behind."

Nate brought up the rear. He deliberately rode
slow until a fifty-foot gap separated him from the
rest. When he came to a cluster of cabin-sized boulders, he reined in among them, swinging down and
shucking his Hawken from the saddle sheath. Then,
keeping low, he worked his way to the lowest boulder, flattened, and crawled to where he had an un-
obstructed view of the slope he had just climbed.

Now all Nate had to do was wait. Whoever was
back there was bound to show themselves. He hoped
it wasn't hostiles.

Some whites were fond of saying that the only
good Indian was a dead Indian, but Nate wasn't one
of them. He didn't hate Indians just because they
were Indians. He'd married a Shoshone woman, after
all, and been adopted into her tribe. He dressed more
like an Indian than a white. And he was so bronzed
by the sun that, were it not for his beard, he could
pass for an Indian.

Long ago, Nate had learned an important lesson.
The red man was really no different than the white.
Oh, each had their own customs, and they wore different clothes and lived in different dwellings and
spoke different languages. But when all that was
stripped away, the red man and the white man were
a lot more alike than either was willing to admit.

Another lesson Nate learned was that, just as with whites, there were good Indians and there were bad Indians. There were Indians who were kind to one and all, and Indians who would slit the throat of an Indian from another tribe as readily as they would slit the throat of a white man.

Movement below brought an end to Nate'e reflection. He rose on his elbows to better see the four warriors who had emerged from the trees and were climbing toward him.

"Damn."

Nate didn't need his spyglass to tell they were Blackfeet. And there was nothing the Blackfeet liked more than to count coup on whites.

Dueling Fingers

It was rare to see Blackfeet so deep in the mountains. Rare, too, to see such a small number. Usually their war parties were made up of thirty or more warriors. Nate suspected the four were a hunting party; they had spotted Ryker and the Woodrows lower down and were waiting for a chance to kill them or steal their horses, or both.

Nate racked his brain for a way to avoid bloodshed. A parley was out of the question. The warriors were apt to attack the moment he showed himself.

Reluctantly, Nate settled the Hawken's sights on the warrior in the lead and thumbed back the hammer. He curled his finger around the rear trigger and pulled it to set the front trigger. Then, his finger around the front trigger, he took a deep breath to steady his aim.

The four Blackfeet abruptly halted and stared intently up the slope.

To Nate, they appeared to be looking right at him, or at the boulders he was in. He couldn't imagine how they had spotted him, as low to the ground as he was. Then he realized they weren't staring at him; they were looking at something to his right. He raised his cheek from the Hawken and received a shock.

Tyne Woodrow had come around the boulders, apparently spotted the Blackfeet, and drawn rein. There she sat, smiling sweetly down at them.

Alarm coursed through Nate. He doubted the Blackfeet would kill her. But they might decide to take her back with them to raise as one of their own. He placed his cheek to the Hawken, but he didn't shoot. All four warriors had bows. If they should send a flight of arrows up the slope, a shaft might hit Tyne.

Nate stood and moved into the open. Stepping close to Tyne, he said without taking his eyes off the Blackfeet, "Don't move. We are in deep trouble."

"Mr. King!" Tyne said cheerfully. "I wondered where you got to. I thought maybe your horse threw a shoe, so I came back to look for you. Who are those Indians?"

"They are Blackfeet and they don't like whites."

"Why wouldn't they like me? I've never done them any harm. My mother says that so long as we are nice to people, they will be nice to us. And Indians are people, too."

Nate's regard for the girl soared. "Sometimes nice isn't enough."

"Should we go talk to them and ask what they want? My father says that Indians like to trade."

"We'll stay put."

"I have some pretty ribbons for my hair. One is green and one is yellow and another is the most wonderful blue. Do you think they would like ribbons for their wives or their sisters?"

Nate almost laughed at the notion of pacifying the implacable Blackfeet with a few paltry ribbons.

"Oh, look! The one with the big nose is coming toward us. He's quite dashing except for his nose."

Nate tensed. The warrior in the lead was indeed

climbing. Nate raised his Hawken, then realized the warrior had not done the same with his bow. Suspicious of a trick, Nate lowered his rifle again.

The other Blackfeet weren't moving.

Tyne turned out to be a little chatterbox. "My goodness, they have fine buckskins. And look at how their hair shines. What do they use to make it shine like that?"

"Some Indians slick their hair with bear fat," Nate offhandedly mentioned.

"Goodness gracious. Indian girls too? I couldn't do that. I like my hair loose so the wind can blow it, but mother nearly always makes me wear a bonnet."

"Hush. I must concentrate." Nate could ill afford a distraction.

"I'm sorry. Am I talking too much? Mother says I do that. She scolds me about it. But how do we get to know people if we don't talk to them?"

"Hush," Nate said again. A thought struck him and sent a shiver of apprehension down his spine. It could be there were more than four Blackfeet, and the others were flanking him.

The lead warrior came to a halt within easy arrow range. Most Blackfeet were highly skilled with a bow and could hit a target the size of a man's head from a full gallop.

Nate tried to read the warrior's expression. He saw the man's eyes widen slightly, and he glanced over to see Tyne beam and wave.

"How do you do?" she called down. "We are pleased to meet you."

"You don't listen very well," Nate said.

"You said not to talk to you. You didn't say anything about not talking to them."

"Don't talk at all. Let me handle this."

"All right. But if you want, I will get my ribbons out."

"Just sit still and be quiet." Nate stepped in front of her horse. If arrows did fly, he could shield her with his body.

The lead warrior was still staring. He appeared to be in his thirties or maybe his early forties. He had high cheekbones and an oval chin. A single eagle feather was in his hair. He gave no indication of what he was thinking or what he was going to do.

Nate took a gamble. Leaning his Hawken against the boulder, he raised both hands so the Blackfoot could see them. Then he clasped them in front of him with the back of his left hand to the ground. It was the hand sign for "peace."

Most tribes used sign language. Some tribes used signs that others did not, but overall the hand gestures were remarkably consistent. So much so, that a Blackfoot or a Piegan, who lived up near Canada, could communicate with a Comanche from down Texas way.

The warrior didn't react.

Nate waited. When half a minute went by, he repeated the gesture and added another. He held his right hand in front of his neck with his palm toward the Blackfoot, then raised his index and second finger toward the sky and curled his thumb over the other two. It was the sign for "friend."

The warrior swiveled and called down to the other Blackfeet in the Blackfoot tongue. Then he took the arrow from his bow and slid it into his quiver. The bow went over his shoulder. All this to free his hands. Quickly, his fingers flowed with practiced skill.

While Nate was not a natural born linguist like his

wife, he was well versed in sign, and he followed the gestures easily. No one knew exactly how many hand signs there were. Many hundred was the common consensus, but Nate believed it might be over a thousand. Even so, a lot of words that whites took for granted were not among them.

In sign the Blackfoot said, "I called Black Elk. I Blackfoot. I count many coup. I want know you called."

"I called Grizzly Killer," Nate signed. It was the name the Shoshones called him, bestowed on him long ago after he slew his first griz. He waited for Black Elk to sign in reply but the warrior was staring at Tyne. Nate elected to come right out and ask why the warriors were following them. Since there was no hand sign for the word "why," he had to go about it another way. Raising his right hand shoulder-high with his palm toward Black Elk and his fingers and thumb splayed apart, he twisted his wrist several times. It was sign language for "question." He continued by signing, "You follow us?"

Black Elk pointed at Tyne. "Girl have sun hair."

Nate thought he understood. Tyne was probably the first blonde Black Elk ever set eyes on. Since Indians nearly always had black hair, to Black Elk her yellow curls must be extraordinary.

"Question. You trade her?"

Nate was taken aback.

Tyne chose that moment to ask, "What are you two doing with your hands? Talking?"

"It's called sign language."

"Oh. I remember hearing about it. Can you teach me? I would love to talk to Indians that way. I bet I would learn a lot of new things."

"Do you remember me asking you to shush?" Nate noted that the other warriors hadn't moved.

That was encouraging, but the whole situation could change for the worse if what he signed next angered Black Elk. "No trade girl."

For the longest while Black Elk sat still, staring at Tyne. Then he signed, "Give ten horses."

Nate hid his unease. By Blackfoot standards, Black Elk was offering a lot. It showed how much Black Elk wanted her. "No," he signed.

"Give twenty horses."

"No."

"My heart big. Give fifty horses."

Nate had never heard of such a thing. Fifty was wealth beyond measure. "Yes, you have big heart." Which was the same as saying Black Elk was being incredibly generous. "But whites no trade people. No people before time. No trade people time in front. No trade people now." In effect, Nate was saying that whites never had and never would trade one of their own.

"Maybe we take her."

Nate scowled. There it was. Black Elk was threatening to abduct her if they didn't come to terms. He signed, "Question. You want war with whites?"

Black Elk's hands stayed at his side.

"You take girl, whites be mad. Whites take war bonnet. Many whites come Blackfoot country. Whites bring many guns. Whites fight. Whites kill. Many Blackfeet die."

"Blackfeet maybe kill many whites," Black Elk signed.

Nate did not press the issue. He had given the warrior something to think about. But the truth was, he was bluffing. The whites would not go to war over one girl. Whites were taken captive all the time and nothing was ever done about it. Oh, sometimes the bereaved families arranged a trade. But once a white woman was taken she was generally considered lost for good.

Tyne coughed to get his attention. "You two are doing an awful lot of finger wriggling. What about?"

"They're hunting. He asked me if I'd seen any elk."

"We saw a cow elk yesterday. They sure are big. A lot bigger than deer. They remind me of horses. Has anyone ever put a saddle on an elk and tried to ride it?"

"You are doing it again."

"Doing what?"

"Does your mother ever gag you?"

Tyne giggled. "I'm sorry. I can't help it. I'm excited. The only other Indian I ever met was a Delaware and he was as tame as a kitten. These are wild Indians, aren't they?"

"As wild as Indians come."

"And yet they are being nice and not trying to kill us. Why don't we ride down so I can see them close up."

"No."

"I promise not to talk much."

"The answer is still no."

"You're not being very friendly to them."

Nate focused on Black Elk. The warrior was signing again.

"Question. You trade part yellow hair? I give horse. I give blanket. I give knife."

It took Nate a few moments to realize what Black Elk was asking. "I'll be damned," he blurted.

"Mr. King! My mother says we shouldn't ever use that kind of language. When my brothers do it, she makes them wash their mouths out with soap."

Nate drew his bowie knife. "Bend your head down."

"Whatever for?"

"I need a lock of your hair. Do you mind?" Nate started to reach up but Tyne recoiled.

"This is most peculiar."

"It's not for me. The Indian with the big nose has taken a fancy to you. If we give him a lock, he and his friends will go away and leave us be."

"And if I would rather keep all my hair right where it is?"

"Then they will bide their time and jump us when we least expect. Instead of settling for your hair, they might take *you*. And your mother and father and brothers and sister might lose their lives protecting you."

"Oh my." Tyne gazed at Black Elk. "I suppose I should let you have it, then. I would die before I let harm come to my family. But take it from the back of my head so I don't have to see."

"Good girl. Now bend down." A single stroke was all Nate needed. Cupping the snippet, he left his Hawken where it was and descended a dozen steps. He held his hand out so Black Elk could see the golden lock, and beckoned with the other.

Black Elk dismounted. Head high, shoulders squared, he came up the slope. He didn't sign or say anything. He accepted the lock, held it almost reverently in his own palm, and stroked it with a fingertip.

"Question. We friends?" Nate signed.

Black Elk smiled at Tyne, said something in the Blackfoot language, and headed back down. He placed the lock of hair in his pouch. Rejoining his companions, he climbed on his horse. Without a backward glance the four warriors wheeled their mounts and made for the trees.

Nate felt tension drain from him like water from a sieve. He climbed to the boulders and reclaimed his Hawken.

"Why did you look so worried?" Tyne asked. "You had me thinking they might be out to hurt us when all they wanted was a piece of my hair."

Nate saw no reason to tell her the truth.

"If you don't mind my saying so, Mr. King, that was awful silly. My mother would say you didn't use your head. She says that a lot about men."

"Does she, now?"

"Oh, yes. She says men need women to tell them what to do."

"How did your mother get so wise?"

"I don't know. It comes naturally to her, I guess."

Hate and Love

The pass was a wagon-wide gap high on the divide. Once through it they would be on the west side of the Rockies. Rock walls reared on either side. Normally, the gap was in deep shadow, but they reached it when the afternoon sun was at its zenith.

Nate still brought up the rear. He didn't trust the Blackfeet. They were devious enough to let him think they'd left, only to sneak back and pounce when he was off his guard.

The others filed into the pass ahead of him. All except one. Nate was surprised to find Edwin Ryker waiting for him.

"Where did you get to earlier? You disappeared for a while."

Nate remembered a story he heard about how Ryker lost his ear. "I checked our back trail."

"You don't say." Ryker smirked. "That isn't what Tyne told me. She says you ran into some Indians and gave them a lock of her hair. Her mother is fit to be tied."

"I'll explain to Erleen and Peter when we stop for the night."

"What I would like to know," Ryker said much too casually, "is which tribe they belonged to."

"Does it matter?"

"It does to me. Were they Cheyenne? Nez Percé? Utes? Which?"

"I suspect Tyne already told you."

Ryker hissed in anger. "You're damn right she did. They were Blackfeet. And only four bucks." He jerked on the reins to swing his sorrel back down the mountain. "Take the Woodrows on by your lonesome. I'll catch up when I can."

"No you don't." Lunging, Nate grabbed the sorrel's bridle. "You're staying with us. They hired you, not me."

"Let go." Ryker sought to break away. "I have a score to settle with those sons of bitches." He went to raise his rifle.

In the blink of an eye Nate had a pistol in his hand. "I am not one for threats. But if you try to ride off, I'll shoot you out of the saddle. Rile the Blackfeet and the Woodrows might suffer."

"What about *me*?" Ryker was livid. "How about *my* suffering? Who do you think did this?" He snatched off his floppy hat and smacked the jagged scar tissue. "It was Blackfeet. A war party caught me when I was camped near the Missouri River. I thought for sure I was a goner. But do you know what those devils did?" He didn't wait for Nate to answer. "They made me run a gauntlet. Instead of filling me with arrows and lifting my scalp, they stripped me naked and made me run between two rows of painted bucks armed with war-clubs and knives. Do you have any idea what that is like?"

As a matter of fact, Nate did. But he held his tongue.

"I was never so scared in my life, and I am not ashamed to admit it. There were twenty of them on either side, screeching and whooping and waving their weapons. I didn't think I would live to reach the end. But when their leader prodded me with a lance, I took off like a spooked rabbit. I held my arms over my head but it didn't do me much good. I hadn't gone ten steps when it felt like every bone in my body was broke." Ryker stopped, and trembled.

"You don't need to tell me this."

Ryker didn't seem to hear him. "And God, the pain! I hurt so bad, it is a wonder I didn't pass out. Then one of them hit me on the shin and I tripped and fell to my knees. That was when a tomahawk caught me on the side of my head." Ryker ran his fingers over the hideous scar. "Took off my whole damn ear. But in a way it was a good thing."

"How could that be good?"

"Because it brought me out of myself. It sank in that I was going to die unless I did something. Something they didn't expect." Ryker chuckled a strange sort of chuckle. "I went to my hands and knees, as if I was about to collapse, and they stopped beating on me. Maybe they figured I was done for, what with all the blood and my ear torn off, and all. But I tricked the bastards! I pushed between two of them and lit out of there like my backside was on fire."

"And you got away," Nate stated the obvious.

"It wasn't easy. Some of those bucks were fast, damn fast. But I ran and I ran and somehow or other I outlasted them. They still might have caught me, but I found a hollow tree to hide in. They didn't think to look in it and I heard them go right on by. I was never so glad of anything in all my born days."

"You were lucky." Nate knew of other frontiersmen who hadn't been. Only three men, as far as he was aware, ever ran a gauntlet and survived. He was one of them.

"Ever since that terrible day, I've made it a point to kill every Blackfoot I come across. So far my tally is seven. That doesn't count the three squaws I caught last winter out gathering firewood—" Ryker stopped.

"You killed women?"

"So what? They were Blackfoot and that was enough." Ryker glared down the mountain. "Now you want me to let four of those vermin get away? You ask a lot. You and me aren't even pards."

"All I care about are the Woodrows," Nate told him. If Ryker only killed one or two of the Blackfeet, the rest might go fetch friends.

"All right. All right." Ryker swore. "I gave my word and I took their money so I reckon I have to see it through. But just so you know. I don't appreciate you keeping it to yourself." He gigged his sorrel toward the gap but abruptly drew sharp rein. "What the hell? What are you doing there, you old biddy?"

Aunt Aggie came out of the pass. "Watch your mouth, Mr. Ryker. I am a lady and you will treat me as such."

"And if I don't?" Ryker taunted.

"I will cut you some night when you are asleep. Cut you down low so that you can forget ever having children."

"I'm shocked. I thought ladies don't do things like that."

"Some ladies have claws."

Ryker snorted. "As for kids, who wants them? Raising a pack of brats isn't one of my ambitions."

"Nice man," Aunt Aggie said as the frontiersman swung past her and on into the pass.

Nate kneed the bay over. "Did you mean what you said about cutting him?"

"At my age it is a waste of what precious time I have left to squander it saying things I don't mean."

"You are a hoot, Aunt Aggie."

"And you aren't one of the children, so Aggie will do. Or Agatha if you are of a mind."

They followed after the rest. She kept glancing at him and cleared her throat but didn't say anything.

"What?" Nate prompted.

"Tyne told me what you did. I suggested she not tell her parents, but she did anyway. Erleen is fit to scratch your eyes out over that lock of hair. She thinks you had no right."

A shadow passed over them and Nate glanced up. He glimpsed a bald eagle with its pinions outspread go soaring off on the air currents. "I suppose I would feel the same in her shoes."

"You had to give them the lock?"

"They wanted all of her."

"Oh. Damn."

"Don't let Ryker hear you swear. He'll think you are less of a lady than ever."

Aggie chuckled, then sobered. "Erleen will still be mad. I love my sister dearly, but she can be a lunkhead at times. We've never been all that close. It's the age difference. I am nearly twenty years older than she is." Aggie chuckled louder. "Erleen was not supposed to happen. Our parents were considerably surprised when our mother found out she had a new loaf of bread in the oven."

"I have never met a woman who talks like you do."

"Open and frank? It comes with age. I hate to admit

it, but when I was younger I was a lot like Erleen.
Stuffy and snooty and convinced I had all the answers. Then I lost my Harold after thirty-eight years
of wedlock. My oldest son went off to visit Europe,
and stayed. My youngest took up with a woman of
loose morals and under her influence wanted nothing
more to do with me." Aunt Aggie sighed. "That was
when I woke up. When I realized that not only did I
not have the answers, I didn't even know the right
questions."

"I'm sorry," Nate said.

Aunt Aggie's face grew haunted with memories.
"It's not me. It's life. We get so set in our ways that it
never occurs to us that our ways might not be the
way things really are. I took it for granted my husband would live as long as I did, and his heart up and
gave out. I took it for granted my sons loved me so
much they would never up and leave me alone in this
world. But that is exactly what they went and did."

They were well into the pass. Shimmering dust
particles, raised by the others, hung suspended like
so many tiny fireflies.

"Now I don't know what to think," Agatha went
on. "Except that I still have my nieces and my nephews. They adore me and I adore them, and I will be
there for them when they need me, even if it kills me.
Family is everything."

Nate studied her. "Is that why you're here? For
Tyne and her sister and brothers?"

"And for Sully. He's Peter's brother, but he was as
close to me as if he were my own." Agatha paused.
"Sully always treated me nice. He was quite the
backwoodsman, that one. Could live off the land if
he had to. He knew all the wild creatures and their
habits, and which plants were safe for people to eat.

He told me once that he learned from watching the animals. If a plant was safe for an animal, it was safe for us. Smart of him, don't you think?"

Nate knew better, but he didn't interrupt.

"Sully brought me venison from time to time, and we would sit and have wonderfully long talks." Her lips pinched together. "It worries me that we haven't heard from him."

"Peter and Erleen should have come by themselves and left the children home with you."

"We're a family. My boys aside, when one of us is in trouble, we do what we can."

"This isn't the East."

"Meaning we don't know what we have let ourselves in for? But we've managed to get this far without mishap."

"Have you forgotten the Blackfeet? That could have ended badly." Nate sighed. "It is not the same here as back there. The animals are different. The plants are different. *Life* is different. Thing are not as tame. They call this the wilderness for a reason. It is wild and dangerous. And unless a person knows exactly what they are doing, their bones will be picked clean by buzzards."

"My goodness. And I thought I had become a bit of a cynic."

"I am telling you how it is." Nate leaned over and touched her arm. "Be extra careful from now on. Keep watch over the children at all times. Once we are over the divide we are in unexplored country. We could run into anything. Anything at all."

"You're scaring me."

"Good."

"Besides, I thought you said you have been here before. That hardly makes it unexplored."

"I was through this area once, yes, years ago. A few other whites might have passed through, too. But it's never been fully explored. It's as wild as wild can be, and it can bury you."

Aunt Aggie coughed and then smiled. "I am beginning to understand why Mr. Ryker speaks so highly of you. Your woman—what did you say her name was again, Winona?—is very fortunate to have you for her man."

The far end of the pass drew near. The others were waiting. Erleen was saying something to Ryker and Ryker didn't look happy.

"You said Winona is a Shoshone, correct?"

Nate nodded.

"Why did you marry her? Her being an Indian, and all."

"I never expected a question like that from you."

"No. Please. Don't misconstrue. I don't hate the red race just because they are red, like so many of our kind do."

"I married Winona because I love her. Because I care for her with all my heart and all my soul. She is the zest in my veins and the spring in my step. You could say she is the very reason I breathe."

"Oh my. That was practically poetical. I bet you have a work or two by Byron in that library of yours."

Nate grinned. "As a matter of fact, I do."

The pass widened, and they were out of it. Below spread a spectacular panorama of peaks and valleys. Mountains so high, they plunged many of the valleys in near perpetual shadow. Mile after wild mile of country left largely untouched by the hand of man since the dawn of creation. The vast unknown, literal and true. Gazing out over it gave Nate King a rare ripple of goose bumps. He couldn't say why but he felt a sudden unease.

"Your precious Sully couldn't have picked a more godforsaken spot," Ryker said to Peter and Erleen.

"He wanted somewhere where there was plenty of game," Erleen said.

"His own Garden of Eden, as he liked to call it," Peter added.

Ryker shifted in the saddle toward Nate. "Well, Blackfoot lover? You have been here and I haven't. Which way? West? Southwest? Northwest? Where is that sandstone cliff Sully mentioned?"

"Southwest," Nate said after some hesitation.

"Oh, hell. You don't remember it all that well, do you? We could end up searching for a month of damn Sundays and not find the jackass."

Erleen bristled. "Mr. Ryker! I will ask you for the final time to curb that cursing of yours. Must I constantly remind you there are children present?"

Ryker gestured at the spectacular sweep of majesty and mystery below the divide. "Lady, do you see that down there? Do you have any idea what we are in for? Because I promise you that before this is done, my cussing will be the least of your worries."

Nate didn't say anything. Ryker was right. It could be none of them would get out of there alive.

Horror

One lock was not enough.

Black Elk thought it would be. But after he held the wonderful yellow curls in his hand and felt how soft the hair was and marveled at how the sunlight turned the yellow to gold, he wasn't content. He wanted more than one lock. He wanted the whole head, and the girl that went with the head.

The others listened to his appeal, but Black Elk could tell Mad Wolf was the only other one as eager to continue tracking the girl. Mad Wolf was always eager to kill whites. Mad Wolf was always eager to kill anything.

"I say we let them go," Small Otter declared. "They gave you the hair you asked for. To kill them now would be bad medicine."

"You see bad medicine in everything," Black Elk said. "If a cloud passes in front of the sun, to you that is bad medicine."

Mad Wolf and Double Walker smiled.

"And we will not make war on the women," Black Elk went on. "We will not kill Golden Hair or the old one or the other two. Only the men, so we can take their guns and horses."

Double Walker said, "And so you can take Golden

Hair, as you call her, back to our village. What will Sparrowhawk and your other wives say? You have not asked them if they want to raise this white girl as their own."

Black Elk grunted. He had four wives. Among the Blackfeet only a poor man had one wife. Warriors rich in horses and possessions had as many wives as they could support. The leader of their band had five. "They are my women. They will do as I say."

Mad Wolf grinned and said to Double Walker, "He does not want Golden Hair for a daughter. He wants her for a fifth wife."

"She looks young," Double Walker said.

"I can wait a few winters." Black Elk could wait for as long as need be to make her his wife. No one in his band, no one in the entire tribe, had a wife like her. Several warriors had white women in their lodges but none with hair so yellow. Hers was like the sun. She must be a favorite of the sun god, he thought. She would bring good medicine to his lodge and his people. And at night, under the blankets, he could run his fingers through her hair and—he grew warm at the imagining.

Small Otter was speaking. "There is another matter. This Grizzly Killer. His is a name we all have heard. He is white but he is Shoshone. It is said he has killed more of the silver tip bears than any man, white or red. It is said he has counted many coup."

"Are you afraid?" Mad Wolf sneered.

For a moment Small Otter appeared ready to strike him. Instead he said, "If you truly think I am, we will set all our weapons aside except our knives and you can test my courage."

It was Black Elk's turn to grin. With a bow and arrow they were all about equal in skill. Mad Wolf was best with a lance. Double Walker, so big and so strong, was formidable with a war club. But with a knife Small Otter had no peer.

"Do not take me so seriously," Mad Wolf said. "As for Grizzly Killer, yes, he has counted many coup. They say he has killed Sioux. He has killed our brothers, the Bloods and the Piegans. He has killed Blackfeet. He is a great warrior." His face lit with the passion that inspired him more than any other. "Think of our fame if we kill him."

"Think of *your* fame, you mean," Double Walker said. "You are the one who wants to count more coup than any Blackfoot who ever lived."

"I make no secret of that. We are warriors. Warriors kill. The more we kill, the greater we are. I will be the greatest one day. Our children and our grandchildren and our grandchildren's children will sing songs about me."

"Here he goes again," Small Otter said.

Black Elk held up a hand. "Enough. If Mad Wolf wants to kill Grizzly Killer, I wish him success. My interest is the girl, Golden Hair. But Mad Wolf and I cannot kill the white Shoshone or steal the white girl alone. Are you with us? Are we together in this?"

Double Walker shook his war club. "I am with you."

"Good."

Small Otter scowled. "We have been friends since we were little. We have grown together. We have hunted and played and gone on the war path together. So yes, I am with you. But I want it known I do not think we are doing right. I have a bad feeling."

"You always have bad feelings," Mad Wolf said.

Black Elk slung his bow across his back. "Then we are agreed. We must hurry. The whites are making for a pass high up that will take them to the other side of the mountains. But I know another way. A faster way. We can get to the other side ahead of them and catch them unprepared."

Hurriedly, they mounted. With Black Elk in the lead, they rode south along the edge of the forest until they came to a game trail pockmarked by elk and deer tracks. It led up a long slope to a wall of rock well below the summit. The wall had a break in it, a break barely wide enough for a horse, but it brought them to the other side of the mountain well before the whites could hope to make it through the high pass.

Drawing rein, the four Blackfeet surveyed the maze of peaks and shadowed valleys. All was deathly still, even the wind. Not so much as the chirp of a bird reached their ears.

"I do not like this country," Small Otter said.

"There must be much game," Double Walker remarked.

"And plenty of ghosts."

Mad Wolf rolled his eyes. "Not that again."

"Only a fool is not afraid of ghosts. You know as well as I do that they like forest and rivers. Look below us. What do you see? Forests, and in the distance a river."

"I see smoke," Double Walker said, and pointed.

Rising out of a shadowed valley below were gray tendrils that writhed and coiled like snakes. The valley was thick with timber and dark with gloom thanks to sheer red cliffs that hemmed it on three sides. One of the cliffs had been split long ago by a mighty cataclysm.

"A village?" Small Otter wondered.

"Not enough smoke," was Black Elk's opinion. "It is a campfire."

"We should go see," Mad Wolf proposed.

The game trail wound down into the dark valley. They were just entering the dense forest when Double Walker thrust out a muscular arm. "Look there!"

A dead cow elk lay on her back, her legs wide, her belly ripped open. Ropy loops of intestine and other organs had spilled out, along with a flood of blood, now dry.

"Dead five or six sleeps, at least," Small Otter guessed.

Black Elk leaned down as low as he could to examine the cow elk. "I have never seen a kill like this. See these bite marks? Where something has chewed meat off the rib bone? What animal bites like that?"

None of them could say. They rode on, their bows strung and shafts notched. The stillness of the forest was unnatural, the quiet absolute. The dense ranks of trees could hide a multitude of enemies.

"There are ghosts here, I tell you," Small Otter whispered.

A stream gurgled to their right, but they couldn't see it. Once Black Elk thought he glimpsed a flicker of movement. He didn't like this place, but he didn't tell the others. Mad Wolf and Double Walker would tease him as they teased Small Otter about ghosts.

The smell of smoke grew stronger even as the cliffs seemed to grow higher. When they looked straight up, all they saw were the cliffs and a small patch of blue sky.

"Let us leave this place," Small Otter declared.

Black Elk gave him a sharp glance. As he did, once again he thought he glimpsed movement in the heavy undergrowth. He strained his eyes but saw nothing.

The trail curved, and a clearing appeared. But it wasn't the clearing that caused Black Elk to draw rein in amazement. It was what stood on the other side of the clearing.

Mad Wolf, Double Walker and Small Otter came to a stop to the right and left of him. Their expressions mirrored the same astonishment.

"This cannot be," Double Walker whispered.

"I would ask you to hit me to wake me, but I know I am already awake," Small Otter said.

Mad Wolf made a stabbing gesture. "Are the whites everywhere now? It is one of their wooden lodges."

Black Elk thought he understood. "This is where Grizzly Killer and the others are coming. They must have friends in that lodge."

"We should kill them and wait in ambush," Mad Wolf advised. "Grizzly Killer will ride up and—" He suddenly stopped, his eyebrows arching toward his hair. "Do you hear what I hear?"

From the structure came loud, merry singing. Not good singing, either, but the kind that set the ears on edge.

"It is a woman," Black Elk said.

"She has the voice of a frog," was Mad Wolf's opinion.

At a gesture from Black Elk, they dismounted. Each tied his horse to a tree. Then, bows at the ready, they advanced in a skirmish line, spreading out as they went. They were within a stone's throw when the singing suddenly stopped.

Black Elk halted and the others followed his example. He had seen such dwellings before. Unlike the buffalo-hide lodges of his people, which had flaps for entering and leaving, the lodges of the whites had rectangles of wood that swung out and in. He remembered that the entrances were usually in the middle of the front wall, and sure enough, he saw a rectangle of wood in this wall. He also saw a square opening to one side, covered by a red cloth. Even as he set eyes on it, the red cloth parted and a pale face peered out at them. A female face.

"She has seen us!" Mad Wolf cried.

Black Elk braced for an outcry, for a shriek of warning that would bring armed white men rushing from the lodge. But the woman didn't cry out. She didn't scream. She did the last thing Black Elk expected her to do: she smiled at them. Then the red cloth closed.

"That was strange," Small Otter whispered.

"She showed no fear," Double Walker said.

Black Elk sighted down his arrow at the square with the red cloth. He was sure that was where the white men would show themselves. But to his surprise, the flat wood in the center of the front wall opened and out stepped the white woman. She showed all her teeth, and held what appeared to be long needles and part of a blanket.

Instantly, all four of them trained their bows on her.

"Why is she smiling?" Small Otter wondered.

"She is ugly," Double Walker said. "If she was not wearing clothes, I would take her for a buffalo."

To their utter bewilderment, the woman began to sing.

Black Elk glanced at his friends. It was plain they shared his perplexity. "Be careful," he cautioned. "This might be a trick."

The white woman smiled and sang and was not afraid, not even when Mad Wolf took a step toward her and made as if to shoot an arrow into her belly. "I will spare our ears."

"Wait," Small Otter said uneasily. "I do not like this. What if her head is in a whirl?"

"She must be alone," Double Walker said. "No one else has come out of the lodge."

Black Elk didn't know what to think of the white woman's behavior. He realized that her singing was not really singing at all. She was chanting. But what she had to chant about was as great a mystery as her presence.

"Do I kill this buffalo or not?" Mad Wolf asked.

Black Elk was about to say it would be best if they silenced her when the white woman gazed toward the woods and clasped her arms to her bosom as in great joy. He looked to see what she had seen and his blood turned to ice in his veins. Shock sent him back a step. "Beware!"

The others whirled.

Mad Wolf instantly let fly with his arrow but the thing that had come out of the forest bounded aside and the arrow missed.

"It is a ghost!" Small Otter cried.

Black Elk disagreed. Whatever it was, it was flesh and blood. He snapped his bow up to let his own shaft fly.

"There is another!" Double Walker shouted, thrusting his arm toward a second apparition.

"And a third!" Mad Wolf warned. "Where do they come from? What *are* they?"

"We must flee!" Small Otter exclaimed.

Black Elk refused to run. He had never run from anyone or anything in his life; his bravery was a byword among his people. For him there was one recourse, and that was to slay the things before the things slew them. Accordingly, his bowstring twanged—and the shaft flew wide of his leaping target.

"Behind you!" Double Walker bellowed.

Uncertain whether the warning was intended for him or one of the others, Black Elk started to turn. He was only halfway around when something slammed into his back with such force that he was driven to his hands and knees. He lost his bow. Pain racked him, but not enough to stop him from grabbing for his knife. Before he could jerk it from its sheath, his wrist was seized in an immensely strong hand. A stinging pain in his throat resulted in a warm, wet sensation spreading down his neck and chest. He became unaccountably weak, and pitched onto his side. Something tore at him and he couldn't lift a finger to stop it.

Black Elk saw Mad Wolf and Double Walker, both down and being ripped limb from limb. He saw Small Otter flee toward the white lodge. For a few moments he thought Small Otter would make it into the lodge, but the buffalo woman sprang with remarkable speed and ferocity and buried one of her long needles in Small Otter's eye.

Black Elk's own eyes became wet and sticky with his blood. The world faded around him. The last sound he heard was a gurgling whine that came from his own ravaged throat.

Pinpoints

"Do we go on, or do we stop for the night?"

The question was posed by Peter Woodrow. They had descended a short way from the pass and were winding down a steep slope that severely taxed their mounts. The sun, low in the western sky, cast long shadows that were slowly growing longer.

Nate King gazed to the southwest. In the distance were sandstone cliffs. If his memory served, that was where they would find the valley Sully had mentioned in his one and only letter to his parents. But getting there before night fell was impossible unless they could sprout wings and fly. "I say we find a level spot to make camp."

Ryker overheard, and disagreed. "Why stop when we're so close? When we could have a roof over our heads tonight?"

"I can give you a whole list of reasons," Nate said. "One, our horses are worn out. Two, so are we. Three, we would have to ride for hours in the dark, and you know how dangerous that is. Four, even if we reach the valley, it could take us hours more to find the cabin. Five—"

"All right. All right. You've made your point."

"I agree with Mr. King," Peter said. "My family is

exhausted. You mustn't forget there are women and children."

"I gave in, didn't I?"

"Why are you in such a foul temper, Mr. Ryker?"

"I can give you a whole list of reasons," Ryker mimicked. "But I won't." He gigged his horse.

"A most puzzling man," Peter remarked. "Some days he is as nice as can be. Other days he is mad at the world and everyone in it." Shaking his head, he followed Ryker.

Nate was still at the rear, behind Tyne. He had a crick in his neck from glancing over his shoulder so many times. There had been no sign of the Blackfeet, but he wasn't convinced they had given up.

Someone else hung back, and reined in alongside his bay. "I hope you don't mind my company," Aunt Aggie said. "We never had our chat about readers and reading."

"It will be hard to talk with all the riding we must do."

"Oh, we'll manage."

And they did, off and on. Agatha did most of the talking. About how her mother had read to her when she was barely old enough to toddle. About how she had loved to hear bedtime stories. "Fairy tales and fables were my favorites. I particularly liked the little red hen and the grain of wheat, and Aesop's fable about the fox and the stork."

Nate admitted to liking Bible stories, and tales about great heroes of the past. One of his favorites was "Jason and the Argonauts." As a boy, one of his prized books had been a copy of the work by Apollonius of Rhodes. His father called it an extravagance but let him have it.

"Typical," Aunt Aggie said. "Boys are fond of tales

of derring-do, while girls go for more practical stories."

Nate mentioned that his daughter, Evelyn, most liked "Goldilocks and the Three Bears," and "Jack and the Magic Beanstalk," when she was little. It brought fond remembrances of the many nights he had read to Evelyn and Zach in front of the cozy fireplace in their cabin. Those were glorious times.

Nate missed those days. Life seemed simpler then. When children were young their needs were few, and meeting those needs was easy. But when they grew older, a whole host of new problems arose, and being a good father became more of a challenge. The best a father could ask was that the problems were few and far between, and that they lived through them.

Ryker gave out a yell. He had found a suitable spot to camp for the night. Just in time. The horizon had devoured half the sun.

Sheltered from the wind by fir trees, Nate kindled a fire while Ryker and Peter tethered the horses. Aunt Aggie had Fitch and Harper gather firewood and drag logs over for everyone to sit on. Anora helped her mother fix supper. That left Tyne, who came and hunkered next to Nate.

"My aunt says you did me a favor today."

"Oh?" Nate was concerned that Aggie had mentioned the Blackfeet wanted more than Tyne's hair, but he should have known better.

"Only that you are a nice man and she is glad we ran into you." Tyne smiled. "So am I."

Nate added a piece of tree limb to the fire and the flames spat and hissed.

"Tell me about your girl, Evelyn," Tyne requested. "What is she like?"

"She will be seventeen her next birthday. She likes flowers and pretty dresses, but she can shoot the eye out of a buck at fifty paces, and she can ride like the wind when she has to."

"You sound very proud of her."

"I am. When she was younger, she didn't like the mountains. Her mother and I thought she would move back East one day, but she hasn't talked about doing that in over a year now. I guess she decided the mountains aren't so bad, after all."

"Are they?" Tyne asked.

Nate stared at the encircling veil of darkness. "The mountains are as they have always been. They have beauty, and they have perils. We can admire the beauty, but we must watch out for the perils."

Erleen was suddenly there, her hands on her hips. "I will thank you not to scare my daughter. We have made it this far without mishap. It puts the lie to all those tales about savages behind every tree and beasts behind every bush."

"All it proves is that you and your family have been very lucky. But no one's luck lasts forever."

Erleen patted Tyne's shoulder. "Don't listen to him, dear. He's lived in the wilderness for so long, he has forgotten how to behave in polite company."

Nate resented the accusation, but he bit off a reply. He reminded himself that Erleen Woodrow was used to the tame and peaceful East. He sincerely hoped she made it back there without having to learn that her world and the West were not the same. It could be a painful lesson.

The aroma of boiling stew filled the clearing. Everyone settled down, making themselves comfortable. Nate remarked that if all went well, tomorrow they should learn the fate of Sullivan and his family.

"I pray to God they are all right," Peter said.

"They will be," Erleen predicted.

"I hope we can talk them into coming back with us," Peter remarked, adding for Nate's benefit, "That's another reason I came in person. I would like to convince Sully that enough is enough. He should buy property near mine so we can be like we were before he got it into his head to live in the Rockies."

"He loves the outdoors too much," Aunt Aggie said.

The stew was mostly water with bits of squirrel meat and some flour for thickening, but it was hot and it was filling. Nate poured coffee into his tin cup and sat back on a log to relax, but just as he raised the cup to his lips the night was shattered by a howl to the southwest.

"A wolf!" Tyne exclaimed, jumping to her feet. "I have yet to see one this whole trip."

Nate wasn't so sure. He listened for the howl to be repeated, and it was. A long, high, wavering cry, shrill and piercing.

The next moment Ryker was at his elbow. "Have you ever heard a cry like that?"

"Never," Nate admitted.

"Me neither. It wasn't no wolf, though. And it wasn't a coyote or anything else I can think of. What the hell?"

Other howls rent the night. There was more than one of the beasts, whatever they were.

"Mr. Ryker, you swore again."

"Sorry, ma'am. I will stop cussing when I stop breathing. Until then you'll just have to put up with it."

Erleen looked mad enough to smack him. "I am sorry to say this, Mr. Ryker, but you frontiersmen are a scurvy lot. Some of you, anyway."

"And I'm not sorry to say this, ma'am, but I ride a horse and not on a ship, and my name isn't Blackbeard."

Aunt Aggie chortled.

"Had I known you could be so petty, Mr. Ryker, I would have hired someone else to be our guide."

"Begging your pardon, ma'am, but there aren't many who will come this far in. Bridger would do it, but last I heard, he was guiding wagon trains. Walker would do it, but last I heard, he was in California. Jedidiah Smith went and got himself killed by Comanches. That leaves King, here. You're getting two for the price of one."

"Was that a barb, Mr. Ryker?"

"Perish the thought, ma'am."

Peter broke in with, "As soon as everyone is done eating, we should all turn in."

Fitch raised his face from his soup. "But I'm eighteen. I should get to stay up as long as I want."

"I want to get an early start, son, and we all need rest."

The howling stopped. Whatever gave voice to it had gone quiet.

"We should take turns keeping watch," Nate proposed. "Two hours each. I'll take the first turn. Then Fitch, Harper, and you, Mr. Woodrow. That will leave an hour or so for Edwin."

"Don't call me that. I hate that name."

"Very well, Mr. King," Peter said. "If you feel it necessary."

"I do."

Tyne gave Nate a hug before she turned in. Soon he was the only one not bundled under blankets. Perched on a log by the fire, his rifle across his thighs, he sipped coffee and listened to the night sounds.

And there were a lot. The meat-eaters were abroad. Coyotes yipped. Owls screeched. Occasionally, the roar of a griz announced that the monarch of the land was on the prowl. The screams of mountain lions were rarer yet. Twice, Nate heard howls that he was sure were made by wolves. He didn't hear the strange howls again.

Before long, Fitch took over.

Nate lay on his back with his saddle for a pillow and a blanket pulled to his chin. He gazed up at the myriad of sparkling pinpoints in the night firmament, waiting for sleep to claim him.

Nate was on the verge of dozing off when Fitch whispered, "Mr. King, are you awake?"

"Yes."

"I think something is out there."

Smothering a yawn, Nate rose on his elbows. "I didn't hear anything." He saw only darkness.

"It was there." Fitch pointed to the southwest. "Something moved. I didn't get a good look at it."

Nate stared until his eyes ached. "There's noth—" he began, and stopped. Something *did* move, a flicker of white against the backdrop of black. He sat up and grabbed his Hawken.

"Did you see that?" Fitch breathlessly asked. "What on earth was it? A deer?"

Nate didn't know. He had never seen anything like it: a hunched-over form, as pale as a sheet, that was lightning quick. He would almost swear it was on two legs but that was preposterous. It moved too silently, too swiftly.

"Mr. King?"

Nate threw off his blanket. "I'll keep watch awhile. You turn in."

"That wouldn't be fair. You just laid down."

Of all of them, Nate had talked to the boys the least. Fitch and Harper tended to keep to themselves. They had their father's reserve and were not as open as the girls. But Nate liked them. They were dutiful, decent young men who would soon make their own mark in the world. "I don't mind."

"Whatever you say, sir."

Nate smiled in wry amusement. His own son hardly ever said "sir" to him. Zach was too independent, too much his own person. Nate wished Zach were there now. With his son to back him, he would take on anyone or anything without any qualms.

Nate took Fitch's place on the log. The night had gone quiet, a temporary lull in the beastly bedlam of predator and prey. It sobered Nate to contemplate that at that very moment, scores of meat-eaters, everything from martins to bobcats to wolves to grizzlies, were feasting on fresh, succulent flesh. It made a man thankful for the senses God gave him, and the brains to use them.

Nate refilled his tin cup. His eyes were leaden, his limbs sluggish. He probably should have let Fitch continue to keep watch, but Nate was a firm believer in the old saw that if you wanted something done right, do it yourself. And while Fitch was able enough, the boy lacked Nate's experience.

Half a cup later, Nate was having trouble keeping his chin up when a feeling came over him that he was being watched. He gripped the Hawken and peered into the dark, but nothing moved. Dismissing it as nerves, he went on sipping and struggling to stay awake.

The feeling persisted. Nate set the cup down and stood. His Hawken level at his waist, he warily stepped to the edge of the clearing.

Everyone else was sound asleep. Erleen snored loud enough to be heard in California. The horses dozed.

Nate grinned at his foolishness. He was about to turn back when he thought he saw, at the limit of his vision, a pair of tiny dots, virtually pinheads of light. It took him a few moments to realize what they were. *Eyes*, reflecting the glow of the campfire. Eyes fixed unblinkingly on him. As Nate looked on, a second and then a third pair of dots appeared. There were three of them. He snapped the Hawken to his shoulder even though he didn't intend to shoot, not without knowing what they were. But the instant he raised the rifle, the three pair of dots disappeared, as if they had blinked out of existence, or melted away.

A shiver ran through him. More nerves, Nate thought. Whatever those things were, they hadn't tried to harm him or any of the others.

What were they? Despite Nate's many years in the mountains, despite his familiarity with every animal in the wild, he couldn't say. And he didn't like that. He didn't like it one bit.

Nate hoped he had seen the last of them.

Hidden Valley

From a distance the sandstone cliff did indeed look like a giant red *V*. The cliff was part of a horseshoe ring of stone that cut the valley off from the outside world. The only way in was through the open end of the horseshoe.

As Nate and the Woodrows wound down the last slope, the hooves of their horses pinged on rock. Anyone in the valley was bound to hear them long before they got there.

Ryker, in the lead, held up an arm, bringing everyone to a stop. He bent toward the ground, then straightened and beckoned to Nate. "You need to see this!"

Nate trotted past the others. Tyne grinned as he went past. Aunt Aggie smiled and winked. Peter asked what he thought was the matter, and Nate answered that he had no idea. Which wasn't entirely true. Nate figured Ryker had found tracks of some kind, and Ryker had. But not plural; just one track.

"What the hell do you make of that?"

The print was in a patch of soft earth. Whatever made it had five toes. Not claws or pad, but *toes*. Crooked toes, splayed wide apart. There was no sole or heel. Just the toes and a ridge of callus.

"Someone barefoot, running on their toes," Nate speculated.

"That's what I thought. But look at how those toes are twisted. They aren't natural."

Nate had to agree.

"And look at how deep the toes dig into the dirt. Whoever or whatever made it was either very heavy or has iron leg muscles."

Nate thought of the pale specter the night before, and the eyes gleaming with fire shine.

"I wanted you to see it before the others rode over it." Ryker paused. "I wonder if it has anything to do with those howls we heard."

Nate shrugged.

"I still can't get over Sully Woodrow coming this far into the mountains. What in God's name was he thinking?"

"Peter says he wanted to get away from people."

"Well, he picked a damned good spot. This is as off the beaten track as you can get. His wife must have been fit to be tied. Most women wouldn't like living in the middle of nowhere."

Erleen cleared her throat to call out, "Mr. Ryker, can we keep moving? We have a long ride ahead of us yet, and I, for one, would like to get it over with."

"Sure, lady. Keep your britches on."

"Mr. Ryker!"

Nate lifted his reins. "I'm going on ahead. I'll blaze trees as I go so keep your eyes peeled. Take it nice and slow. If you hear a shot, have the rest wait and you come on alone. We don't want any of them harmed."

"Hell, I don't want *me* harmed. But why this sudden urge to scout around? Do you know something I don't?"

Nate bobbed his chin at the track. "I wouldn't call

it sudden." He went past Ryker and made his way lower. He was on the lookout for more of the strange tracks but didn't see any. Soon he came to the base of the mountain and the valley floor spread out before him. Trees formed an impenetrable phalanx except where a game trail threaded among them.

Nate had only gone a few yards when he drew abrupt rein. Other riders were ahead of them. Hoofprints merged with the trail, coming from higher up but not from the direction of the pass. The horses that made the tracks weren't shod. That meant they were Indian mounts.

Nate thought of the Blackfeet. If it was them, he couldn't begin to explain how they got there ahead of him. It didn't bode well. Drawing his bowie, he cut a notch in a tree for Ryker, then rode on at a walk, his thumb on the Hawken's hammer.

The woods were primeval, as woods must have been at the dawn of time, the pines so closely spaced, the branches formed a canopy that blocked out the sunlight filtered over the towering cliffs. It was like being in a whole new world. Or maybe an *old* world.

Suddenly the bay nickered and shied. Nate calmed it, then spotted the cause: a dead elk, a cow on her back with her innards ripped out. Keeping a firm grip on the reins, he dismounted and moved closer. The stink was abominable.

As best Nate could reconstruct the cow's death, she had been brought down by blows to her legs; both front and rear leg bones were shattered. Once she was on the ground, whatever attacked her had rolled her onto her back and tore at her exposed belly. Her throat, though, was unmarked. That in itself was remarkable. Mountain lions and other meateaters nearly always went for the neck.

Climbing back on the bay, Nate cautiously wound deeper into the valley. He hadn't gone far when he came on another dead animal. This time it was a horse. It had been struck a terrible blow to the head, above one eye, that nearly caved in its skull. The force had popped the eye from its socket, and now the eyeball dangled by its stem.

Nate gave a start. He had seen this particular horse before. It belonged to one of the Blackfeet.

Nate's unease returned. He scanned the woods, but if anything was out there, it was lying low. Riding on, he shifted to keep an eye behind him. The skin between his shoulder blades wouldn't stop prickling.

Somewhere to Nate's right a stream gurgled. He angled toward it. Maybe it wasn't smart to leave the game trail, but the bay could use a drink, and the banks of a stream were prime places to find tracks. Every living creature needed water to live.

The gurgling grew louder, but the trees and undergrowth screened the stream from him until he was right on top of it. Any notion he had of finding tracks was dashed by the thick grass that covered both banks.

Climbing down again, Nate stood guard while the bay drank. Utter silence prevailed; silence so complete, it was uncanny. He listened in vain for the chitter of a squirrel or the warble of a bird.

Behind him, a twig snapped.

Nate spun, every nerve jangling, but nothing was there. He started into the woods but caught himself before he blundered. Whatever had killed the elk and the horse would not hesitate to do the same to the bay. He dared not leave it alone. Backing away, he pulled the bay's muzzle out of the water and forked leather.

Nate returned to the trail. The walls of vegetation became thicker the farther he went. Enclosed spaces never bothered him—but this did. Nate had the bizarre impression he was riding into the gullet of some gigantic beast. Silliness of the first order, but there it was.

Nate shook himself. He passed a pine carpeted with moss. He passed a rotting log amid a profusion of mushrooms. He passed a cluster of thorn apples.

Up ahead, a clearing appeared.

Nate's skin prickled worse than ever. At the edge of the trees he drew rein and said the first thing that came into his head. "I'll be damned."

On the other side of the clearing stood a cabin. The front door was shut. Red curtains covered the window. From the roof rose a stone chimney but no smoke climbed into the sky.

The cabin and the clearing were so quiet and still that Nate was almost sure no one was there. But he didn't take chances. He rode with every sense alert, the Hawken to his shoulder.

"Is anyone there?"

No one responded. The door stayed closed, the curtains were undisturbed.

Nate was halfway there when he noticed splotches of red mixed with the green of the grass. It was blood. Dry blood. A lot of blood, spilled not all that long ago. Newly dry blood always had a bright sheen and this was as bright as could be.

Nate drew rein. The logical conclusion was that the four warriors had killed the people in the cabin.

Or been killed by them. But if that was the case, where were the bodies?

"Is anyone home?" Nate called out.

There was no answer.

Nate walked up to the front door and tried the latch. The door wasn't bolted. It swung in on creaking leather hinges.

"I'm a friend. Don't be afraid." Nate poked his head in and smothered a cough. The place had a strange smell. Not a foul odor, as such, but different from the odor of any cabin he had ever set foot in. The cause eluded him. It wasn't tobacco or any food he was familiar with.

Keeping his back to the wall, Nate sidled inside. The room was dark, even darker than the gloom of the forest. He paused, letting his eyes adjust. "I'm a friend," he repeated.

Nate made out a table with benches instead of chairs. Over by the fireplace was a rocking chair. And that was about it, save for cupboards and pots and pans.

A dark doorway yawned to his right. Nate went over. "Anyone in here?" He poked the door with the Hawken. The *thunk* of metal on wood seemed unnaturally loud. Within were empty shelves and a metal hook speckled with dry blood, suspended from the ceiling. It was a pantry.

The strange smell was stronger.

Nate closed the pantry door and went back outside, grateful for the fresh air. He checked the ground. The grass near the door was flattened, the earth scuffed and scraped. There weren't any clear prints, but it was enough to tell him that someone—or several someones—used the cabin regularly. He opened the door and poked his head in again. The floor and the furniture were free of dust, which they wouldn't be if neglected.

Nate hastened to the bay. He disliked leaving it untended. The unease he'd felt since entering the valley hadn't gone away.

The logs used to build the cabin weren't trimmed. Here and there stubs poked out. One was long enough to wrap the reins around to keep the bay from wandering away.

Nate stared up the trail. Peter and Erleen would arrive soon. He used the time to prop the front door open with a broom and to open the curtains to clear out the smell. Logs stacked next to the fireplace simplified kindling a fire. He also lit several candles scattered about. He wanted the place to be as cheerful as he could make it. He was thinking of the girls, of Anora and especially Tyne.

Nate debated what to do about the blood. A shovel suggested a solution. He dug dirt from the side of the cabin and sprinkled it over the red splashes and spots. Next, he put coffee on to boil.

The Woodrows still hadn't shown up. Nate went to the door. He hoped they were all right. He hadn't heard shots or screams, and he doubted the Blackfeet could take them completely unaware.

The wait tested Nate's patience. He paced back and forth in front of the cabin. He paced back and forth in the cabin.

Once, when he was outside, rock clattered against rock off in the trees. The sound wasn't repeated.

The high cliffs lent an oppressive gloom to everything. Nate noted that the valley continued for another quarter of a mile past the cabin, ending where the cliffs met. It was worth a look-see but it would have to wait. He wanted to be at the cabin when the others got there.

Nate's unease grew. The last time he had felt this way was in Apache country. He couldn't shake the notion that at any moment something might rush out at him. He told himself he was being ridiculous, but it didn't help.

Over an hour passed.

Nate thought hot coffee would soothe his nerves. Several cups were in the cupboards but he felt compelled to use his own. He went out to the bay and opened the parfleche. As he reached in, a twig snapped.

Nate spun, leveling the Hawken, and caught movement in the trees near the cabin. "Who's there?"

No one answered.

Nate could make out a vague two-legged shape. "I know you're in there. Show yourself."

The figure moved, but only a couple of steps.

Nate's thumb and trigger finger twitched, but he didn't shoot. "If you are one of Sullivan's family, I won't harm you. I'm here with Peter and Erleen. They should show up shortly."

"Don't shoot! I'm coming out!"

It was a big-boned woman in a dress and a bonnet, clasping two long knitting needles and a partially knit shawl. She smiled an anxious smile, as if she couldn't make up her mind whether he was truly a friend, or a foe.

"I am with Peter and Erleen Woodrow," Nate repeated, lowering his rifle. "I mean you no harm."

The woman came closer. "Intery, minstery cutery corn, apple seed and apple thorn."

"What?"

"You're not really you, are you?"

"Lady, I am as real as you are," Nate assured her.

"You think I am really real?"

"Of course."

"If all the world were water, and all the water ink, what should we do for bread and cheese? What should we do for drink?"

"Why do you keep saying nursery rhymes?"

"Why do you not say them?" The woman laughed.

"Are you Philberta?" Nate asked. She answered the description he had been given.

"This little pig went to market, this little pig stayed at home."

"Talk sense, will you?"

"This little pig had roast beef, this little pig had none."

"Cut that out. And tell me. Are you Philberta or aren't you?"

"To be honest, sir, I'm not sure anymore." She laughed again, a sad sort of laugh. Then she swept a knitting needle over her head and cried, "Let's see which of us is real!"

And with that she attacked him.

Vanishings

The wild gleam in her eyes, her wild talk, had warned Nate she was unbalanced. He was ready when she lunged. Screeching, Philberta stabbed the knitting needle at his eyes, her face twisted in pure hate.

Nate swept the Hawken up, one hand on the barrel and the other on the stock, blocking her blow. She was strong, this woman. The force jarred him onto his heels. He could have shot her but instead he sought to reason with her, saying, "I'm not here to harm you! Get that through your head."

"Liar!" Philberta cried, and came at him again. She had the second knitting needle in her other hand, low against her side.

Nate backpedaled. He hadn't counted on this sort of reception. He'd figured that the survivors, if any, would be overjoyed to see him and learn their relatives were on the way. "Stop it!" he commanded. But she paid him no heed. He dodged a needle to the neck, shifted, and evaded a stab to the groin.

Philberta crouched to try again. She was quick as well as strong, and unless Nate did something, fast, she was bound to skewer him.

"For the last time, I'm not your enemy!"

Philberta grinned. "Jack be nimble, Jack be quick. Jack, jump over the candlestick."

"Why do you—?" Nate began, and got no further. She came at him, thrusting high and low, and it was all he could do to stay out of her reach.

"Stand still, consarn you!" Philberta's bosom was heaving and a sheen of sweat dampened her brow. "You are worse than a jackrabbit." She feinted and went for his groin, but he sidestepped.

Nate had taken as much as he was going to. Springing back, he leveled the Hawken. "The next step will be your last."

"One, two, buckle my shoe." Philberta raised both needles. "You might get me but I will get you."

"Philberta! What on earth?"

At the shout, Philberta turned. Shock replaced the hate, shock so profound, she shook from her bonnet to her shoes. "I must be dreaming."

Ryker and the Woodrows had arrived. Ryker was smirking in amusement, but the Woodrows gaped in horrified disbelief.

Erleen had found her voice first, and now spoke again. "Put down those knitting needles. That man is a friend of ours. He helped us find you."

"Erleen? Peter?"

"It is indeed us, my dear."

"Am I seeing things again?" Philberta had forgotten about Nate. She ran a sleeve across her face, and swayed. "It must be the strain. I've finally snapped."

Erleen was clambering from her horse. "Listen to me, sister-in-law. We're not figments. We're real. We were worried when we didn't hear from Sully and you, so we came west."

"Oh God." Philberta looked at Nate, her eyes widening. "What have I done?"

Erleen hastened up, her arms spread wide. "Calm down and give me a hug. I've missed you and the others so much."

Nate tensed. He half feared Philberta would bury the knitting needles in Erleen, but to his relief Philberta let the other woman embrace her. Suddenly Philberta gasped, and stiffened. Her eyes rolled up in their sockets until only the whites showed. Then, with a loud groan, she collapsed and would have fallen if Erleen hadn't been holding her.

"Peter! I need help!"

Nate was closer. He quickly slipped an arm under one of Philberta's. "It's good you came along when you did."

"What did you do to her?"

"*Me?*" Nate said. "I was friendly and polite. But she went into a frenzy and tried to kill me."

The others were rushing to help, all except Ryker, whose smirk had broadened. Peter took over for Nate. Fitch and Harper also helped. Nate opened the door and they carried Philberta inside. Anora and Tyne came after them.

"Where is everyone else?" Erleen asked, glancing about. "Sully and the boys aren't here."

"We must set her down," Peter grunted. "She's as heavy as an ox."

"Peter!"

"Well, she is."

The comment made Nate wonder how she was eating so well when the pantry was so bare. Here he'd been worried the family had starved to death. But if Philberta was any example, they didn't miss a meal.

"Where are the beds?" Erleen asked.

Only then did Nate realize the cabin had no bedroom. Nor were there any blankets spread on the floor for bedding. Where did the woman sleep? he asked himself.

"Fitch, fetch blankets off our horses," Erleen directed. "Anora, find a pot, fill it with water from the stream, and put it on to boil. We'll make some tea. Harper and Tyne, I want you to sit here with your aunt while your father and I have a look around."

Nate went out, nearly colliding with Aunt Aggie, who was about to enter. "They can use your help in there."

"Oh, I am sure Erleen has matters well in hand. My sister would make a fine general." Agatha stepped away from the door as Anora bustled past carrying a pot. "I best stay out of their hair."

Nate placed the Hawken's stock on the ground and leaned on the barrel. "So tell me. What is Philberta like when she isn't trying to stick knitting needles into someone?"

Aunt Aggie didn't grin as he thought she might. "Perhaps you should ask Erleen. I've never been all that fond of Philberta and it might taint your opinion."

"You and she don't get along?"

"Oh, she's always been civil enough. But I have long believed Sully could have done better."

"Better how?"

Agatha checked that no one was near. "Less bossy, for one thing. I've always thought marriage should be a fifty-fifty proposition. But Philberta is a lot like Erleen. They snap their fingers and their husbands jump."

"Yet it was Sully who dragged her and their boys west," Nate noted. "He must do some snapping himself."

"I've wondered about that. If Philberta had no yen

to come, Sully wouldn't." Agatha shrugged. "But that's neither here nor there. The real reason I have never gotten along with her is that she treated me coldly. From the very first day I met her, nearly twenty years ago, she gave me the impression she wouldn't mind one bit if I were to be run over by a carriage."

"Didn't you say Sully and you were close?"

"So?"

"So maybe Philberta was jealous. Some women refuse to share their husband's affections with anyone, even a doting sister-in-law." Nate smiled to lessen the sting.

"There's always that, I suppose, although I suspect her dislike of me ran deeper. Anyway, what's done is done. What is important now is to find out where Sully and their sons got to. It's very strange they're not here if she is."

"You want strange? She kept reciting nursery rhymes, as if I were five years old."

Aunt Aggie chuckled. "That's Philberta, all right. She has always been fond of them. When her boys were toddlers, she read them rhymes by the hour. I thought she overdid it, but Sully didn't object, so I never said anything."

Edwin Ryker picked that moment to walk up and hold out a hand to Agatha. "I'll take the rest of my money now."

"I beg your pardon."

"What?" Nate said.

"Didn't you know?" Ryker asked him. "Aggie here is paying for my services. She paid for the horses and supplies, too. Peter and Erleen couldn't afford to do it on their own."

"I am glad to help them," Agatha said.

"You hired me to bring you to Sullivan. Half in

advance and the other half when I got you here. That was our deal." Ryker bobbed his chin at the cabin. "Well, here we are. I'll take the rest of what is owed me."

"Are you a simpleton, Mr. Ryker?"

"Ma'am?"

"Because I know I'm not. I paid for you to bring us here and take us back. Safely, I might add."

"There was no talk of back too. Hell, you told me you might stay with Sully's family a month or so. You can't expect me to wait around that long."

"You will if you want to be paid."

Ryker jabbed a finger at her. "Now you listen here, lady—"

Whatever else he was going to say was cut off by a shriek of terror from the direction of the stream.

"Anora!" Aunt Aggie cried.

Nate was already running. He half expected the Blackfeet were to blame. But when he came to the bank, Anora was on her knees at the water's edge, staring aghast at the woods on the other side. "Why did you scream?"

"Something!" Anora gasped. "I didn't get a good look at it. But it was watching me, and its face was terrible."

Nate plunged across the stream and up the other bank. He charged into the vegetation, the brush crackling to his passage. He went a dozen strides and spotted a bulky form off through the boles. It was four-legged, whatever it was. An elk, he thought, or maybe a mountain buffalo. But it turned out to be neither.

There was the snap of underbrush, and the horse Black Elk had been riding came barreling out of the shadowy greenery to stand in front of Nate and whinny. He grabbed the rope bridle to keep it from running off. As he did, it occurred to him that this might be a ruse, that the Blackfeet were using the horse as bait to lure one of them within arrow range.

The way Nate had the events worked out in his head, the Blackfeet had stumbled on the cabin and killed Sullivan Woodrow and his three sons. That explained the blood in the grass and Philberta's hysterics. And now the Blackfeet intended to kill the rest of them.

"Mr. King?" Aunt Aggie called. "Are you all right?"

"Get your niece back to the cabin!" Nate pulled the horse toward the stream. To his surprise it didn't resist. In fact, the horse acted eager to be in his company.

Ryker was waiting on the bank, and at sight of the horse, he swore. "That there belongs to a redskin. What the hell is it doing here?"

"You wanted to tangle with those Blackfeet I met," Nate reminded him. "Could be you will get the chance."

"It's one of theirs?" Ryker's flinty features gleamed with vicious glee. "And here I was ready to light a shuck."

Nate waded the stream, pulling the horse after him. That the Blackfeet let him take it surprised him. Horses were immensely valuable to them, the most prized possessions of any warrior.

"They must have followed us without us catching on," Ryker said.

"I think they got here ahead of us."

"How? They didn't beat us through the pass or we would have seen sign." Ryker scanned the forest, his thumb on his rifle's hammer. "Not that it matters.

Just so they show themselves. I aim to blow out their wicks, every last one of the bastards."

Nate passed him. "Cover me," he said, and quick-stepped toward the cabin. Ryker backed along after him. Aggie and Anora were almost there, Aggie carrying the pot Anora brought to the stream.

Nate was surprised that no war whoops pierced the gloom and arrows didn't whiz out of the air. At the cabin he handed the reins to Ryker. "Wait with the others until I get back. Don't let anyone come outside."

"Where will you be?"

"Prowling around," Nate said. But not on horseback. The dense brush made it too easy to be picked off. Sprinting around the corner, Nate angled into the woods. He was in among the trees before a feathered shaft or heavy lance could find him. Crouching, he scoured the undergrowth. If the Blackfeet were there, they blended in so well they were invisible.

Working his way with consummate care, Nate headed toward the junction of the high cliff walls. The forest was as dark and quiet as ever. He searched for tracks, human or animal, but didn't find any. That in itself was peculiar. There should be wildlife, what with the stream. If he didn't know better, he would think the wild things shunned the valley.

"Mr. King! Mr. King! Where are you?"

Nate drew up short. That was Tyne. He had told Ryker not to let anyone venture outdoors. Reluctantly, he pivoted on a heel and jogged back. She was a good twenty feet from the cabin, alone and unarmed, as defenseless as a fawn. "You shouldn't be out here."

"Mother and Father sent me to find you. Aunt

Philberta has come around, and Mother wants you to hear what she has to say."

"Where's Ryker?"

"Mr. Ryker found a bottle in one of the cupboards. He is at the table, drinking."

Nate's blood boiled. Taking her hand, he ushered her inside, making sure to close the door after them. On a blanket on the other side of the room lay Philberta, Peter and Erleen on their knees beside her. Anora was making tea. Aunt Aggie, Fitch and Harper whispered together in one corner.

Ryker was at the other end of the table, and had just taken a swig. Smiling crookedly, he beckoned. "Care for a sip? It's brandy, not whiskey, but it goes down smooth just the same."

Nate walked over and did the last thing Ryker expected.

He hit him.

Tale of Woe

Nate King was seething mad. He'd seen too many people die because they were careless. All it took was one mistake. He was doubly incensed because Ryker had lived in the Rockies almost as long as he had and was well aware of the dangers. Yet Ryker let Tyne go out by herself.

But as mad as Nate was, he didn't hit Ryker in the mouth, or even the face. He hit him in the chest. The blow sent Ryker tumbling from the bench.

"Mr. King!" Erleen cried.

Cursing, Ryker scrambled to his feet. "What the hell was that for?"

"I told you not to let anyone go out."

Ryker blinked, then glanced at Tyne. "I told them not to. But her mother sent her to find you."

"Why didn't you come look for me instead?"

"The mother asked the girl. I'm not their nursemaid. If they won't listen, it's on their shoulders."

Nate would have torn into him again if not for Aunt Aggie. Suddenly she was between them, her hand on Nate's chest.

"No more. Please. It's upsetting everyone."

The Woodrows were appalled by the violence. Erleen had her hand to her throat. Anora was wringing her hands. Peter wore a stern look of disapproval. But what cut Nate the deepest was the bewilderment on Tyne's face. He stepped back. "Sorry," he said—to them, not to Ryker.

"My word!" Erleen exclaimed. "That was uncalled for. You acted like a savage."

Nate directed his anger at her. "When will you get it through your head? This isn't Pennsylvania. You can't let Tyne go wandering out alone."

"I only sent her to call you. She wasn't to go far, and we are right here."

Nate shook his head in disgust. Some people were too thickheaded for their own good. He was about to say as much when when Philberta stirred and groaned. The rest quickly gathered around her, with the lone exception of Ryker. He sat on the bench and glared.

Nate went over to the others.

Philberta had opened her eyes and was gazing about in confusion. She licked her thick lips with the pink tip of her tongue, then weakly said, "Where? What?"

Erleen gently squeezed her hand. "Everything is all right. You are in your cabin in the Rockies. Peter and I came to find you after we hadn't heard from you for so long."

"Erleen? Is it really you?"

"It's really and truly us. All of us. We brought the whole family. Plus my sister."

"Agatha too?"

It could be Nate's imagination but Philberta didn't sound happy about Aggie being there.

"She's always been fond of Sully. You know that. She was gracious enough to foot the bill for much of the cost for our expedition."

Philberta's eyes roved the half circle of anxious faces and fixed on Agatha. "Thank you."

"You are welcome, dear."

Peter bent low. "Tell us. Where is my brother? Why aren't Sully and your boys here?"

"Give me a minute," Philberta said. "I can't think straight. I am all confused."

Nate didn't see what she had to be confused about. To him, she was stalling. But then, his wife always said he had a suspicious nature.

"Take your time," Erleen told her. "We are here for you. Whatever you want, you only have to ask."

"I can't believe all of you have come so far on our behalf."

Peter said, "The Woodrows stick by one another, come what may. Sully would be there for me if I needed help." He gripped her wrist. "Where *is* he?"

Erleen, appalled, slapped her husband's arm. "Let go of her! Can't you see she is in a bad way? The poor dear has been through some sort of ordeal."

"That I have," Philberta said softly. "An ordeal such as none of you could possibly conceive."

"Enlighten us," Aunt Aggie said.

"I lost a baby."

Nate was as shocked as the Woodrows. Out of the corner of his eye he saw Ryker chuckle, and he almost went over to hit him again.

"A baby!" Erleen exclaimed. "Philberta! At your age?"

"I know, I know. It's been fourteen years since our last. Since Blayne was born. We certainly didn't want any more. But shortly after Sully finished building our cabin, I found I was in the family way. I was scared, terribly scared, as I wouldn't have a doctor or even a midwife to attend me."

"I don't blame you. I would have been scared too."

"But Sully was confident everything would be fine. You should have seen him. So caring. So devoted."

"That's my brother for you," Peter said proudly.

Philberta wanly smiled. "But confidence isn't always enough. Especially when we started to go hungry."

"What are you talking about?" Peter asked. "Sully is the best hunter I know."

"He never had trouble keeping food on our table back in Pennsylvania, that's for sure," Philberta replied. "There was so much game. Deer, rabbits, squirrels, grouse, pheasant, woodchucks." She paused. "But it turned out not to be the same here."

"Nonsense. These mountains teem with wildlife. We saw a fair amount of animals with our own eyes."

"So did we, at first. But it wasn't as easy as Sully thought it would be. The black-tailed deer aren't as plentiful as the whitetails used to be. And the smaller game was the same."

"What about elk?" Erleen asked.

"They are a lot higher up, and wary. There are squirrels and rabbits, but not nearly as plentiful as we were used to."

Nate could have told them. A lot of Easterners assumed it was as easy to fill the supper pot west of the Mississippi as it was east of the Mississippi. But they were mistaken. Yes, there was a lot of wildlife, but not as much. Yes, deer were deer, but blacktails were a lot more wary than their eastern cousins, and a lot harder to hunt and bring down.

"Sully did his best. And our boys helped. Norton

was eighteen. Liford seventeen. Blayne fourteen. They could all hunt. They went out with Sully day after day, but too often all of them came home empty-handed."

"Preposterous."

"Let her talk, Peter," Erleen said.

"With five mouths to feed and a baby on the way, it got so we were missing meals. We had to eat whatever we could. Sully told us to watch the animals. Whatever they ate would be safe for us."

Nate frowned. There it was again. The ridiculous notion that was so widespread people took it as gospel.

"We got sickly, though. I was worst of all. Probably because of the baby. Sully made me stay in bed. He had the boys do the chores, the sweeping and cooking and whatnot. But I grew weaker and weaker." Philberta stopped, and shuddered. "Finally the day came." She looked up at Erleen and tears filled her eyes. "It was a girl. She was stillborn."

"Dear God."

"We buried her out back and got on with our lives. Sully was so sweet. But he was worried too. We all were. Between him and my sons, they pretty much hunted all the game in our valley. They had to go farther and farther afield, and left me alone for days at a time."

Erleen stroked her brow. "You poor dear."

"Then Sully shot a bull elk. They butchered it and brought the meat home and for a while we had plenty to eat. Thick, juicy steaks, smothered in mushrooms and greens. They dried a lot of the meat for jerky. We thought the worst was over." Philberta took a deep breath. "Then Norton disappeared."

"No!"

"He told us he had found Indian sign. He was going to show Sully the next day, but that evening he went out and didn't come back. We never saw him again."

"Surely there was some sign of what happened to him?" Peter asked.

"Sully took Liford and Blayne and they searched for Norton for days. But they didn't find him."

Nate had a few questions that needed asking. He interrupted with, "What about that Indian sign?"

"Pardon?" Philberta craned her neck and rose slightly to see him. "Who are you? I've never seen you before."

"This is Mr. King," Erleen said. "A mountain man who helped us find your cabin."

"Oh. What was it you wanted to know?"

"You mentioned Indian sign. Did your husband and your other sons find any when they were out?"

"No. None." Philberta sniffled. "We were all so sad, losing Norton. Sully made us stay close to the cabin. And pretty soon practically all our elk meat was gone. They had to go hunt again, and that was when Liford vanished."

Erleen gasped. "Your middle son too?"

"It gets worse," Philberta said. "Sully and Blayne searched and searched but couldn't find a trace of him. Sully was heartbroken. Two of his boys, gone. He insisted Blayne stay with me at all times."

Peter impatiently demanded, "But where are Sully and Blayne now? Don't tell me they disappeared as well?"

"I'm coming to that."

"Hush, Peter, and let her tell her story."

Philberta closed her eyes, her face a portrait of sorrow. "We began to feel as if we were being watched.

Sully was convinced that something, or someone, was spying on us. Blayne said he felt the same at times. I felt it least, but I wasn't outside as much as they were."

"The savages, I bet," Peter growled. "They killed Norton and Liford, and they were after the rest of you."

"I won't tell you again to hush."

Philberta's lower lip quivered. "We had no food left. It got so we were reduced to eating mushrooms and weeds—"

"How awful!" Erleen said.

"But Sully didn't give up. He went off after another elk. Blayne stayed home. Along about the third day, he went to the stream for water and never came back."

Peter shook a fist. "Those damned heathens! Mr. King, Mr. Ryker, we must find out which tribe is to blame."

"Honestly, Peter."

"Sorry, dear."

"Go on, Philberta."

Philberta struggled to compose herself. "When Sully came back from the elk hunt empty-handed and found that Blayne was gone, something changed inside of him. He ranted and raved about taking revenge. I tried to reason with him. I pleaded. I got down on my knees and begged. But he wouldn't listen. He filled his powder horn and ammo pouch and went off to find the slayers of our children."

"Good for him!" Peter declared.

A tear trickled from Philberta's right eye. "He never came back. I waited and waited, praying hour by hour. Finally I couldn't deny the truth any longer.

I was all alone in the middle of these vast mountains, left to fend for myself without a weapon or a mount."

Nate couldn't stay silent. "Wait. Where were your horses?"

"Gone. Before Norton disappeared. That's partly why we didn't just saddle up and leave."

Erleen held her sister-in-law's hand to her bosom. "The horror of it all. You have my utter sympathy, my dear. But take heart. We are here now, and no further harm shall befall you."

"I am glad you have come."

"We will take care of you, dear," Erleen said. "We brought two pack horses with plenty of food."

Peter nodded. "And we have Mr. King and Mr. Ryker. They know these mountains well and will keep us well supplied with meat."

Ryker took a swig of brandy. "Maybe Mr. High and Mighty will hunt for you. But not me. I've heard enough. I'm leaving."

"What are you talking about?" Erleen asked

Upending the bottle, Ryker smacked his lips and wiped his mouth with his sleeve. "Haven't you people been listening? Hostiles killed your precious Sully and his boys. They will kill us if we stay. The smart thing to do is pack whatever you want to take and get the hell out of here while we still have our skin."

Erleen turned. "I am tired of asking you to watch your language around my children."

"And I am tired of you asking." Ryker wagged the empty bottle. "Don't any of you have a lick of sense? Do you all want to lose your hair? Because I sure as hell don't. I'm not staying a single night in this cabin, or this valley. If we leave within the hour we can be shed of it by sundown."

Aunt Aggie straightened. "You keep forgetting, Mr. Ryker. Abandon us, and I won't pay the rest of the money."

"Lady, at this point I don't give a good damn about being paid. I care about my hide."

"You are despicable," Erleen said.

Ryker pointed the bottle at Nate. "Don't just stand there like a lump. Tell them, damn it. You know I'm right. If they don't leave, they're all going to die."

Specters

"Are you sure we can't talk you out of this?" Peter Woodrow asked.

Edwin Ryker, astride his sorrel, shook his head. "Not a chance in hell. And before your missus starts in on me again, I have cussed since I was ten and old habits are hard to break."

Aunt Aggie squinted up at the sun, which was well past its zenith. "At least stay the night, Mr. Ryker. I promise you there will be no hard feelings."

"Maybe not on your part, lady, but there are on mine. It's wrong of you not to pay me the rest of the money I'm due."

"We have been all through that."

Ryker swiveled in the saddle toward Nate. "The offer to ride out with me still holds."

"I'm staying," Nate said.

"What for? To be turned into worm food like Sullivan and his boys? Whether it's the Utes or some other tribe, they've made it plain they regard this valley as theirs and they don't like trespassers."

Erleen tried a last appeal. "Give us a week, Mr. Ryker. A week to search for Sully and the others. Then we can all leave together. Is that too much to ask?"

"It is for me." Ryker scratched the scar on the side of his head. "I've been Injun shy ever since I lost my ear."

Tyne put a hand on Ryker's stirrup. "Please don't go. We don't want anything to happen to you."

For a moment it looked to Nate as if Ryker was about to change his mind. Not that Nate blamed him for wanting to fan the breeze. Four people had disappeared without a trace. That usually meant they were worm food.

"That's sweet of you, girl. But my ma didn't raise lunkheads. I am doing what I think is best for me."

"Keep your eyes peeled for those Blackfeet," Nate cautioned. If the warriors were still there. Finding Black Elk's horse had given him grave doubts.

"Don't you think I won't," Ryker assured him. "I'll be damned if I'll fall into their infernal hands twice." He gigged the sorrel, and without a backward glance or a wave, trotted across the clearing. Soon he was lost to view around a bend in the trail.

"I wish he hadn't done that," Peter remarked.

So did Nate. Although they didn't see eye to eye on a lot of things, Ryker was a good shot and handy in a scrape.

"Well," Erleen said, as if that summed up the state of affairs.

Aunt Aggie cleared her throat. "Anora, Tyne and I will work on supper while you tend to your sister-in-law."

"And the boys and I will strip the horses and put them in the corral out back," Peter said.

Nate didn't offer to help. Someone had to keep an eye on the woods.

Cradling the Hawken in the crook of his elbow, he began a circuit of the clearing. He noticed how rapidly the shadows were lengthening. Thanks to the high cliffs, dark would fall sooner than normal. And with the night would come—what?

Edwin Ryker was annoyed. Annoyed at the Woodrows and annoyed at himself. But he hadn't exaggerated when he said he made it a point to fight shy of any and all redskins.

Years ago, before he lost his ear, he had traipsed all over creation, not caring one whit about hostiles. Like a lot of whites, he tended to look down his nose at them, to regard them as little better than animals. His attitude had been let them try to harm him and he would show them what white men were made of.

Then a strange thing happened.

Ryker met a Crow girl. He liked her and she liked him, and the next thing he knew, they shared a lodge. The Crows were friendly to him. Maybe not as friendly as the Shoshones, but since he had taken one of their own as his woman, they treated him as a brother.

Four winters Ryker spent with the Crows. The best four years of his life. He cared for that Crow girl as he had never cared about anyone, and when she was slain, he was crushed.

It happened in the fall. The Crows went on the last buffalo surround of the season. Scores of the great shaggy brutes were slain, and afterward, as they always did, the women went in among the fallen buffs to skin and butcher them. But one of the bulls wasn't dead. It reared and plunged a horn into the belly of his woman, ripping her open from hip to hip.

She was a long time dying.

Ryker sat with her hand in his and comforted her

the best he could, which, under the circumstances, wasn't much comfort at all. When she died, so did something inside of him. He was never the same again.

The years drifted by. Ryker met and loved other women, but it was never the same. When the trapping trade dwindled, he took to serving as a guide and scout. He would never get rich at it, but the work agreed with him, and between jobs he drank. And drank. And drank.

Then came the fateful day Ryker was riding along the Missouri River, on his way back to the mountains after a visit to some Mandan friends. He blundered into a Blackfoot war party and paid for his blunder with his ear. Ever since, Ryker spent many a night tossing and turning and sweating. He lost his ear not once but a thousand times.

No one ever guessed his secret: that when it came to Indians, he had lost some of his courage, as well. To one and all he put on a brave front. The mention of hostiles made him scoff. The mention of the Blackfeet made him laugh with scorn. He hid his secret so well that no one ever suspected.

And now he had gone and run out on those damnable Woodrows and Nate King.

Ryker sighed. They should have paid him. Whatever befell them now was on their shoulders. He had done his part. "If they die it's their own fault," he said to the dense greenery.

And someone snickered.

Ryker drew rein. It came from his left, so low as to make him wonder if he'd heard it. But he was sure he had. He trained his rifle on the trees. A minute went by, but no one appeared. Since he was only half a mile from the cabin, he wondered if Fitch or Harper, or both, had followed him. "I am not amused," he said, hoping to draw them out.

There was no reply.

Puzzled, Ryker tapped his heels against the sorrel. The sun was low in the west, about to dip below a sandstone cliff. Already, an early twilight was creeping across the valley floor.

Determined to put the valley behind him by nightfall, Ryker brought the sorrel to a gallop. He was too savvy to ride it to exhaustion; he went another mile, then slowed to a walk again.

The sun was almost gone when Ryker came to the bottom of the mountain crowned by the high pass that would take him over the divide. He dared not risk the long climb in the dark. He would have to wait until morning.

Ryker climbed a few hundred yards, just to be out of the valley. A ridge afforded an ideal spot to camp. He could see in all directions. Off in the distance gray tendrils of smoke rose from the cabin chimney. He stripped the sorrel, gathered firewood, and kindled a fire. Then he spread out his blankets, sat propped on his saddle, and munched on pemmican. Around him, night descended.

Ryker was troubled. A tiny voice pricked him, warning he had made a mistake. He refused to listen. All that talk about Sully and his sons who vanished was to blame. He shut them from his mind.

The soothing crackle of the fire and the peaceful quiet of the mountain helped Ryker to relax. He thought of Bent's Fort, his first stop on his way east. He would stock up on the few provisions he needed and maybe strike out for St. Louis to treat himself to a week of tawdry delights.

His eyelids grew heavy. His chin dipped, but he

raised it again. He wasn't quite ready to sleep yet. He stuck a piece of pemmican in his mouth and was chewing contentedly when it hit him that it was *too* quiet. By now the meat-eaters should be abroad. By now the night should be alive with howls and yips and screeches. But there was nothing, nothing at all.

Ryker shifted and gazed out over the valley. It was black as pitch. A yellow point of light was visible when the wind stirred the trees. Light from the cabin window, he reckoned. It was comforting to think other people were there but not so comforting to realize it would take hours to reach them if he had to get to them in a hurry.

Ryker cursed. He hadn't put coffee on to brew because he did not want to stay up late. Now he reconsidered. Maybe it would be best to keep watch all night, catch a few hours sleep early in the morning, then strike out for the high pass. He was trying to make up his mind when the sorrel whinnied.

Instantly, Ryker was alert. He put a hand on the pistol at his waist. The sorrel had its head up and its ears pricked and was staring down the slope. Ryker looked and listened, but if something was there it was too far off for him to hear. Or—and the thought chilled him—it was moving too silently for him to hear.

Ryker cursed again. "I am turning into an old woman," he scolded himself, and forced a chuckle.

The flames weren't as high as he wanted, so he added a log. He added another. And yet a third. The circle of firelight grew until a good twenty feet of rosy light kept the black of night at bay.

"That's better," Ryker said to the sorrel. He shifted to make himself more comfortable, and crossed his legs.

Ryker stared at the distant light from the cabin

window and thought of Nate King. They argued a lot, but King was one of the few people he respected. Not because King always tried to do right by others. That amused Ryker. The way he saw it, every man should look out for himself, and the rest of the world be damned.

No, Ryker respected Nate King because King was tough. As tough as they came. How someone could be considerate *and* tough at the same time was a puzzle Ryker had yet to unravel. He would never come right out and bring the subject up because King would—

A twig snapped.

And the sorrel was staring down the slope again.

Taking his rifle, Ryker rose and moved to the edge of the firelight. He stood for a long while without hearing anything. But twigs didn't snap on their own.

The sorrel had lowered its head, so Ryker went back to the fire and added another branch. He told himself a deer or an elk was to blame. Or maybe a bear or a mountain lion. But they rarely ventured close to a fire.

Ryker wondered if the hostiles were stalking him. Few Indians attacked at night, though. Not because they deemed it bad medicine, as some whites believed, but because they didn't have the eyes of cats, as some whites also believed, and couldn't see in the dark any better than whites could.

Something rustled in the trees.

Whirling, Ryker raised his rifle. He strained his eyes until they were fit to pop out of his head. Finally he stepped back and grinned at his silliness. He was letting every little thing spook him.

"Damn me, anyway." Ryker sat back down. In all his years in the wild he rarely had an attack of the spooks. After he lost his ear he was a wreck for a while, but that—

Ryker caught movement in the trees, a pale form moving almost too swiftly for the eye to follow. He snatched up his rifle again and stood. The sorrel was staring in the same direction, so it wasn't his imagination. Something *was* out there.

More rustling brought a nicker from the sorrel.

Ryker glimpsed another pale streak. There were two of them, and they were circling his camp. He broke out in a cold sweat. Wedging his rifle to his shoulder, he thumbed back the hammer. The *click* was reassuring. Whatever was out there, let them show themselves and he would blow them to hell. One thing he never was squeamish about was killing.

Then one of the things uttered a low sound, a sound unlike any Ryker ever heard. Part growl, part laugh, it seemed to come from both an animal throat and a human throat at the same time.

Ryker's mouth went dry. He wished one of the things would come out where he could see it. They weren't Indians, that was for sure. No Indian ever made a sound like *that*. He remembered tales he'd heard of ghosts and haunts and ghouls, tales he'd always dismissed as nonsense. But what if they weren't?

On both sides of the clearing pale shapes suddenly flitted between trees. Ryker swung his rifle toward one and then the other, but he couldn't quite make out what they were. He held his fire, wanting a clear shot.

Then the thing to his right stopped and stood stock-still, staring back at him. It stood on two legs.

"Who the hell are you?" Ryker demanded. "What do you want?"

The one on the other side stepped into sight, but well back from the firelight.

"Damn you! Say something!"

Ryker smothered an impulse to shoot. Let them come closer. They would find out they weren't lead-proof.

The one on the right gave vent to another low growling laugh.

Ryker couldn't make sense of their antics. They weren't trying to hurt him. All they were doing was standing there. Almost as if they wanted to draw his attention. But the only reason for them to do that was to distract him.

From behind him came a stealthy scrape.

Ryker spun. He saw the third pale form clearly; it was coiled a yard away, about to spring. Shock slowed his reflexes. He pointed his rifle, but the thing leaped and smashed the barrel aside as the rifle went off. Then it was on him, ripping and rending. He fell back, as much from horror as the blows. He was aware the other two were bounding toward him, and he desperately clawed for his pistols.

The things were incredibly quick. They were on him before he could squeeze off a shot. He fell with them on top. Blood was everywhere. His blood. A maw ringed with teeth swooped toward his throat.

Edwin Ryker screamed.

Death Gasp

Nate King came up off the bench as if hurled by invisible hands. He was at the window in three bounds. Parting the red curtains, he peered out into the night, the domino in his hand forgotten.

"What on earth?" Aunt Aggie said. She, Anora and Tyne were still at the table, dominoes spread in front of them.

"Didn't you hear that?"

"Hear what, Mr. King?" Tyne asked.

A shot, Nate was about to say, but didn't. It might worry them. "I'm not sure," he hedged.

Aunt Aggie's elbow brushed his. "You can tell me," she whispered.

Before Nate could answer, they both heard something else. Faint and far off, it wavered on the wind like the ululating howl of a wolf. Only it wasn't a howl. It was a scream, a very human scream, a scream of terror.

"God in heaven!" Aunt Aggie breathed. "Who could that be?"

Nate had an idea, but he stayed silent.

"Should we go investigate? Maybe we can help."

"By the time we got there, it would be too late."

Besides which, Nate wasn't about to go rushing off in the dark.

"What are you two listening to?" Tyne asked.

Nate closed the curtains. Aggie spared him having to lie by lying herself. "A coyote, child. A harmless coyote. Let's get on with our game, shall we? Your mother will want to tuck you in soon. It's getting late."

Erleen and Peter were over by the fireplace, conversing in low tones. Fitch and Harper were sitting on their blankets playing cards. Philberta was asleep. She tossed and turned a lot, and from time to time she mumbled unintelligibly.

Nate reclaimed his seat. He matched a six with a six, and folded his arms across his chest to await his next turn. Behind him, propped against the wall within easy reach, was his Hawken. He tried not to think of the shot and the scream, but they echoed again and again in his mind.

"Are you all right, Mr. King?" Anora asked.

"Never better." Nate swapped glances with Aggie.

Tyne was deciding which domino to play. "I want to hear more about your daughter."

"She's a lot like you," Nate said. But it wasn't entirely true. Evelyn had an inner strength the Woodrow girls lacked. They were sweet and kind and polite, but if put to the test, if confronted by a hungry bear or a hostile, they were apt to run where his daughter was more likely to put a bullet into whatever or whoever was out to do her harm.

"Does she like dolls? I have four. One I like a lot, but Mother wouldn't let me bring it. She said it would only get lost or dirty and I could go without until we get home. But I miss it. The doll's name is Mindy."

"When Evelyn was little her mother made a Shoshone doll for her," Nate revealed.

All three looked at him.

"Indians have dolls?" Anora said.

"Why wouldn't they? Girls are the same whether they are red or white, and girls like to play with dolls and dress them up and pretend they are people."

A shadow fell across the table and Erleen announced, "Time to end your game. I have let you stay up past your bedtime as it is."

"But no one has won yet," Anora said. "Can't we stay up another half an hour?"

"No."

"Fifteen minutes?"

"Anora Woodrow, you will put away those dominoes and get ready for bed, and I do not want to hear another word out of you. Is that understood?"

"Yes, Mother."

"The wash basin is on the counter. You can change in the pantry."

"Yes, Mother."

Aggie began gathering up the dominoes. "Leave these for me," she told the girls.

Nate slid his across the table. "Care for a cup of coffee?"

"This late? I wouldn't sleep a wink."

The pot on the stove was half full. Nate poured and went back to the table. The family was preparing for bed. The girls were as cute as buttons in their long nightdresses. Tyne's was pink, Anora's blue. Erleen had them kneel and say their prayers, then pulled their blankets up to their chins and pecked each on the forehead.

Fitch and Harper stopped their card game and turned in.

Nate figured it wouldn't be long before the parents and Agatha chased sleep, but all three joined him at the table. "Something on your minds?"

Erleen coughed. "First off, we want to thank you for staying. Mr. Ryker was a terrible disappointment."

"But he was right. It *is* dangerous here. Every minute you stay, you put your lives at risk."

Peter scowled. "It can't be helped. I care for my brother and his boys. I need to know what happened to them."

"They are long dead by now," Nate said bluntly.

"Possibly. Even probably. But we won't know for sure until we find them or their remains."

"You're asking the impossible."

"My wife and I have talked it over and we are in agreement. We intend to scour the valley from one end to the other."

"You might not find anything."

"Unless someone buried them there will be bones, at the very least. The remains could reveal their fate."

"And if we don't find anything?" Nate asked. "How long are you willing to put your family in peril before you decide enough is enough and return to civilization?"

"We have given ourselves a week. If we haven't found Sully or the boys by then, we will pack up and head for Bent's Fort. You are welcome to accompany us."

"I'll see you as far as the foothills," Nate offered. That should be near enough. At the trading post they could hire another guide to see them across the prairie to the Mississippi.

"Your Shoshone friends will wonder what has become of you," Aunt Aggie said.

Just then, Philberta commenced to toss about and mutter in her sleep, her hands clenching and un-clenching.

"The poor dear," Erleen commiserated. "She's suffered terribly. It's a wonder she is still alive."

"One of us must stay with her at all times while the rest are off searching," Peter said.

Nate set down his cup. "The only ones who will do any searching are you and me."

"I beg your pardon? My sons are perfectly capable of lending a hand. And my wife and Agatha have volunteered to help."

"The more of us who search," Aunt Aggie said, "the sooner we can be done and on our way."

"No."

"You overstep yourself, Mr. King," Peter said. "I appreciate your concern for our welfare, but it is my brother who has gone missing, my nephews who have vanished. I have the final say."

Nate sighed.

"My husband has it exactly right," Erleen parroted. "It's our family, our responsibility. If you want to help we will be eternally grateful, but it is ours to do."

Aunt Aggie agreed. "As much as I might like to side with you, Nate, I can't. Family is family. We must always be there for one another."

"You're missing the point."

"Which is?" Peter asked.

"That all of you could end up like Sully and his sons. Do you really want to bury one another? Do you want to bury Tyne and Anora?"

Erleen puffed out her cheeks like an agitated chipmunk. "That was uncalled for. We love them dearly. The last thing we want is for them to come to harm.

Which is why they will stay at the cabin with an adult to watch over them while the rest of us are off searching."

"Then do me one favor," Nate said. "Don't scatter all over. Hunt in a group. You are less likely to be attacked."

"Staying together would slow the search," Peter objected. "We must split up. Work in pairs, say. And everyone will have a gun. That way we will be perfectly safe."

"Mr. King," Erleen took up the argument, "we don't know that Sully and his boys were set upon by hostiles. It could be they were attacked by a wild beast. A grizzly, perhaps. Or a wolverine. I hear they are especially savage. Or maybe Sully and his sons had a mishap. Accidents happen, you know."

Disgusted, Nate stood and took hold of his rifle. "I need some air." He closed the front door quietly, then stood letting the cool breeze play over him. Off up the valley an owl hooted, a commonplace call, reassuring in its normalcy.

Nate walked around to the rear of the cabin to check on the horses. The corral was barely big enough to hold them but it had to do. His bay came over to nuzzle him and receive a few pats.

Since the night was moonless, the valley floor was plunged in gloom. The high cliffs blocked out most of the starlight.

Nate groped along the rails until he was at the gate and verified it was tied shut.

All appeared peaceful, but Nate wasn't fooled. Nowhere was the old saying about appearances being deceiving more appropriate than in the wild. Nothing was ever as it seemed. Tranquil woods might hide painted warriors. The high grass of a scenic mountain meadow might conceal a crouching cougar. A person must always be on his guard.

Nate turned to retrace his steps. He was almost to the cabin when the undergrowth bordering it crackled. Crouching, Nate sought the source.

Mired in murk, something was moving low to the ground.

Nate tensed. No meat-eater would make so much noise. A porcupine, maybe. Or a small bear.

Suddenly the sound stopped.

Nate imagined the animal had caught his scent. In a few moments it would wander away on its nocturnal rounds. But the night stayed silent save for the owl up the valley and the gurgling of the stream.

Nate had never known a porcupine or a bear to stay still so long. They loved to roam and poke their snouts into everything that interested them. He scoured the ground in his vicinity, but only saw a few downed branches and a log.

The next second the log moved.

Nate sighted down the Hawken. It had to be a man. A man who was stalking him. He fixed the sights on what might be the man's head.

Then the figure gasped and said something in a tongue Nate didn't speak but which he was familiar with. Wary of a trick, Nate stayed where he was.

The man crawled closer. Or, rather, *pulled* himself closer, using both of his arms and taking a ragged breath before each pull.

Nate inched forward. The rank smell of blood and urine washed over him. The figure on the ground reached out, and moaned.

Discarding caution, Nate stepped to the man's side and sank onto a knee. "Do you speak the white man's tongue?" When he didn't get an answer, he switched to his wife's. "Do you speak Shoshone?"

A hand clutched at his, the skin hot to the touch.

"You are a Blackfoot, aren't you?" Nate reverted to English again, knowing full well he wouldn't get a reply. He looked for sign of the others, but the warrior was alone.

Coming to a sudden decision, Nate slipped both arms under the man. It was awkward, carrying the warrior and his rifle, both, but he managed. He worked the latch with his eblows and pushed the door open with his foot. Candlelight splashed over his burden and he nearly recoiled in revulsion.

The warrior was a ruin. His left eye was gone, ripped from the socket, a black cavity all that remained. The right eye was so bloodshot, the white of the eye was red. Scratch or claw marks crisscrossed his face and there were bite marks on his throat. One of those bites had severed a vein, soaking his buckskins with blood. It was a miracle the man was alive.

Peter, Erleen and Aunt Aggie were still at the table. Astonishment had rendered them mute, but not for long. Erleen threw herself out of her chair, crying in dismay, "Where did that heathen come from?"

Nate carefully laid the warrior on the floor. Each breath the man took threatened to be his last. "Question?" Nate asked in sign language. "Enemy wound you?"

The warrior tried to reply, but couldn't make his fingers work. He tried to speak, but all that came out of his mouth was a trickle of fresh blood.

"Someone get a glass of water for him," Nate said.

The warrior's red eye swept the room and stopped on Fitch and Harper. Mewing, he thrust his hand at them, then looked at Nate, trying to convey some meaning.

Nate didn't understand, and said so in sign language.

Whatever the warrior was struggling to get across died with him; he arched his body, convulsed, and exhaled his final breath.

Peter, Erleen and Aggie had come over, and Peter asked, "Is he dead?"

"Where did you find that savage?" was Erleen's question.

Aunt Aggie had one, too. "What was he trying to tell you?"

Nate wished to God he knew.

The Smell of Madness

The search commenced an hour after sunrise.

Nate was the first one up. He quietly slipped out to bury the Blackfoot and covered the mound of earth with rocks to discourage scavengers.

Erleen insisted on a big breakfast. Her daughters and Agatha helped cook and bake. They made flapjacks and oatmeal and toast and corn cakes. Peter remarked that it was too bad they didn't have eggs and bacon, his usual morning fare back home.

Nate wasn't going to eat, but the smells were too tantalizing to resist. Especially when he learned they had maple syrup to put on the flapjacks. Once he started eating, he found he was hungrier than he thought. Four flapjacks, a bowl of oatmeal, and two corn cakes later he was full.

It was decided that Aunt Aggie would stay at the cabin with the girls and Philberta.

"Erleen and I will work as a pair," Peter announced. "Fitch and Harper will hunt together, too. That leaves you, Mr. King, to search by yourself, if you are agreeable."

Nate was more than willing. He could cover more ground alone.

Fitch and Harper brought the horses from the

corral. Nate saddled his bay while they threw saddle blankets and saddles on theirs. Everyone had a rifle except Erleen, who was armed with two pistols. It was decided that she and Peter would search on the right side of the stream, Fitch and Harper would take the other side. That left Nate free to roam as he pleased.

The day started off promising enough. A clear sky and the bright sun dispelled some of the gloom that perpetually shrouded the valley floor.

Nate was the last to leave. "Keep the door closed and barred at all times," he cautioned Agatha.

"Don't fret. I won't let anything happen to the girls or Philberta."

"If you need me, fire a shot out the window and I'll come at a gallop. But whatever you do, don't step foot out of the cabin."

"We'll be fine," Aunt Aggie insisted.

Tyne smiled and waved as Nate rode off and he returned the gesture. He stuck to the trail until it brought him to the cow elk with its belly torn open. Bent low, he rode in ever widening circles. He was thirty feet out when he spied a few indistinct prints. Dismounting, he gave them a closer scrutiny. They weren't mountain lion tracks or wolf tracks. They might be bear tracks, though no claws were evident. Or they might have been made by something else.

Nate rode in the direction the prints pointed. For half an hour he threaded through some of the thickest forest he had ever seen. He was constantly ducking to avoid low limbs and skirting logs. Many were covered with moss. It reminded him of the forests along the Pacific coast, which he visited once years ago.

As Nate neared the high cliffs, the shadows deepened. It wasn't even noon, yet he would swear it was twilight. The green of the trees and the grass became a ghostly gray. It lent the illusion he was in a spectral realm. It didn't help that the woods were so still. Wildlife was completely absent.

At last the trees thinned. Ahead reared the rock ramparts. Nate could see the top by craning his head back. He shuddered to think of his fate should the cliff unexpectedly collapse. Tons of rock and dirt would smash down on top of him, crushing him to a pulp.

The vegetation ended short of the cliff, leaving an open space between the trees and the rock face. Nate debated which way to go and reined up the valley toward the junction of the cliffs beyond the cabin.

Nate was acting on a hunch. He didn't have all the particulars worked out in his head yet, but he had enough confidence in his judgment to put his hunch to the test. He hadn't gone twenty yards when a spot of pink and white caused him to draw rein. Curious, he hung by an elbow and one leg, Comanche fashion, and nearly lost his grip and his breakfast when shock hit him like a physical blow. He was used to violence. He had witnessed more than a few atrocities. But *this* was unthinkable.

The pink and white was a human finger, or what was left of it. Chewed pink flesh from the nail to the knuckle and gnawed white bone below. Judging by the fresh condition of the flesh, it hadn't been there long. Since early that morning, Nate surmised. He left it there. Showing it to the others would only sicken them. And they would still insist on continuing the search. They had proven blind to the danger they were in.

The *chink* of the bay's hooves was unnaturally loud. The wind was stronger here at the base of the cliffs, and every now and again a gust would stir the trees and brush.

Nate looked for tracks, but the ground was too hard. Smudges and a few vague prints were all he found. Anything might have made them. But the finger practically confirmed his hunch. The bite marks weren't those of the sharp shearing teeth of a bear or mountain lion or any other meat-eater. They were made by something with strong but blunt teeth, the same as the bite marks on the cow elk, and on the Blackfoot.

Nate didn't have all the pieces of the puzzle worked out yet. The *what*, he thought he knew. The *why*, he had an idea. And if he was right, the horror of it all was beyond imagining. He must get the proof he needed to convince the others quickly, before anyone else fell prey to the creatures responsible.

Creatures was the right word. They were no longer what they had been. They were like beasts, and yet worse than beasts, in that where wild animals killed to fill their bellies, these things killed for the sheer cruel joy of killing. The cow elk proved that. They only ate part of her. A mountain lion or wolves would have eaten her down to the bone.

Ahead, a shadowy spot on the wall brought an end to Nate's pondering. He leveled the Hawken. But it was only a shallow cavity where some of the rock had broken from the cliff. As he rode on he saw more of them.

By Nate's reckoning he was well past the cabin when he came on the first remains. What was once a squirrel was now bones and skins. Farther on was all that was left of a dead rabbit. After that, a fawn and a doe. Both had only been partially devoured.

The rancid stink of decay filled the air. A harbinger of what awaited past a finger of forest that hid the next stretch of cliff. Nate rounded it and drew rein in stunned disbelief.

A virtual carpet of dead things filled the space between the cliff and the woods. Some of the remains were dry and withered, others more recent, a few with flesh almost as pink as the finger. Nate counted parts of four elk and what had to be a dozen deer. It was if the valley had been picked clean of living things and all the bodies brought here.

The reek was abominable. The bay shied, but Nate goaded it on. He tried to avoid the bay stepping on any of the remains, but several times bones crunched under its hooves and once a hoof came down on the skull bone of a doe.

Nate drew rein a second time. Bile rose in his throat as he stared down at the gnawed but still recognizable features of Black Elk. The warrior's glazed eyes were wide in the shock he must have felt at the moment of his death.

Nate could think of only one reason for the Blackfeet to have somehow gotten to the valley ahead of them. Black Elk hadn't been content with a lock of Tyne's golden hair; he'd wanted Tyne. He reckoned the Blackfeet had aimed to spring an ambush. Only the ambushers had been ambushed themselves.

Nate didn't care to share their fate. Constantly scanning the gloom-shrouded vegetation, he neared the end of the valley. Tall pines hid the junction of the sandstone cliffs. He had no idea what he would find, but he certainly didn't expect to come on a cave.

The opening was as big as the Woodrows' cabin. Sunlight barely penetrated. There was enough, though, to reveal the bones and animal forms that littered the cave floor.

Dismounting, Nate edged closer, placing each moccasin with care. He heard nothing to indicate the cave was occupied. They might be crouched in the shadows, waiting to rush out and overwhelm him before he could get off a shot. But nothing came out of the cave except the most awful reek. A stench so foul, Nate covered his mouth and nose. He held his breath for as long as he could and breathed shallow when he had to.

Stopping near the cave entrance, Nate listened. The silence of the tomb prevailed. Acting on the assumption they were in there, he sought to lure them out into his gun sights.

"I've found your lair! Show yourselves!"

Nothing stirred within.

"What's the matter? You killed those Blackfeet. Now try me, and we'll end this."

Continued silence. Nate might as well have addressed the cliff. Poking his head into the opening, he tried to tell how far back in the cave went. An odd buzzing caught his ear, and something small and dark alighted on his cheek. He swatted at it, and a fly took wing. A fly that was just one of hundreds—if not thousands—swarming over the grisliest of feasts. Nate had noticed a few others on the remains he passed, but nothing like this. The newest kills were covered with them. And those not covered with flies were crawling with maggots.

Nate's breakfast tried to climb up out of his stomach.

Ordinary bloodletting seldom bothered him. But this was different; this was slaughter on a scale that shook the soul. He started to pull back, and saw a foot. It jutted out of the black recess, a moccasin, half-on and half-off. He assumed it belonged to another Blackfoot until he realized how white the skin was. "Ryker?" he blurted, and felt foolish for doing so.

Nate had to make certain. Taking a deep breath, he darted into the cave. Maggots crunched underfoot. Flies rose in thick clouds, clinging to his hair and neck and buckskins. One got up his nose. An involuntary sneeze expelled it, and then he was next to the foot. Bending, he gripped the ankle, and pulled to drag the body into the light. The skin had a parchmentlike quality that told him the body couldn't possibly be Ryker. This was an old kill. He kept on pulling anyway.

The dead man, or what was left of him, matched the description Nate had been given of Sullivan Woodrow. Sully's nose was gone and the cheeks had been chewed on, and empty sockets gaped where the eyes should be, but there could be no mistake.

Placing his arm over the lower half of his face to ward off the stink and the flies, Nate backed out. He couldn't take the abomination any longer. Hurrying to the bay, he mounted and headed back the way he came. He was doubled over, wrestling with his stomach, when a rock sailed out of the woods and struck him on the shoulder.

Instantly he brought up the Hawken, but no one was there.

"Not me you don't," Nate said, reining sharply into the trees. He plunged through brush and circled thickets. He looked behind trees. He looked up in trees. But he found no one.

Frustrated, Nate headed for the cabin. He hadn't liked leaving Aggie and the girls alone. The things that slew the four warriors would have no trouble slaying a woman and two girls.

Glimpses of the chimney spurred him on. He came up on the cabin from the rear and slowed as he drew near the corral. The horses still in the corral heard him and had their ears pricked, but when they saw it was him they didn't whinny or stamp.

A low murmur brought Nate to a stop, someone speaking softly in a singsong voice, as if reciting poetry. It took him several seconds to recognize the voice. Puzzled, he quietly alighted and crept into the trees.

Philberta was on her knees next to a small mound of earth. Her back was to him, her head bowed.

Nate stopped. The mound must be the grave of the baby she lost. He was intruding on her private grief. Then he caught the words she was saying.

"Hush little baby, don't say a word. Mama's going to pluck you a mocking bird. And if that mocking bird won't do, mama's going to get a worm for you. And if that worm is covered with dirt, mama will wipe it with her skirt. And if that worm still won't go down, mama will buy a goat from town. And if that goat you don't like, mama will kill it with a spike."

Nate was rooted in place.

"Hey, diddle, dinkety, poppety pet. How I bet you wish we never met." Bending, Philberta patted the mound. "It's not my fault, my dear. Stomachs are stomachs, Sully always said. But now my Sully is dead, dead, dead."

Nate wished he could see her face. He couldn't tell if she was truly expressing sorrow—or something else.

"I have always liked them, you know. Lullabys and nursery rhymes. When I was a girl they were my very favorite things. I always made my mother sing to me before I went to sleep, or else had her read a rhyme. I would have loved to do the same for you."

Feeling foolish, Nate started to back away.

"I would have read to you. Or skinned a kitten and made mittens of the skin. Or stuck a needle in its eye so it would die, and chopped up the meat for kitten pie," Philberta tittered. "Aren't I just the silliest goose? I was never so tight but that I was loose."

Nate froze.

"Birds of a feather flock together, and so will pigs and swine. Rats and mice will have their choice, and so will I have mine."

Dear God, Nate thought.

Philberta abruptly stood. "A fond adieu to sweet little you." She laughed, and merrily whirled, and seeing him, she recoiled as if she had been slapped. "What have we hear, my dear?"

For the life of him, Nate couldn't think of what to say.

"An eavesdropper, I fear."

Nate forced his mouth to move. "I'm sorry to intrude."

"Did you find my Sully?"

"No," Nate lied.

"Or my dear, sweet boys?"

Nate shook his head.

Philberta's hands rose from her waist. In her right hand was a long-bladed knife. "I can't say as I like that one little bit."

Prelude

Nate King thought Philberta Woodrow was about to attack him. She had a certain gleam in her eyes, a gleam he had only ever seen in the eyes of warriors in the fierce heat of battle or in the eyes of wild beasts driven berserk. Instinctively, he leveled the Hawken. "Don't."

Philberta stopped. She trembled slightly, and the gleam faded. "Why, Mr. King," she said, as calmly as could be. "Why are you pointing that thing at me?"

Nate didn't say anything.

"I'm sorry if I acted a little distraught. Visiting Esther's grave always makes me near mad with grief. Surely you can understand?"

"Yes," Nate admitted. He would feel the same if he lost either of his children. They were part of him, given life and form.

Philberta waggled the knife. "As for this thing, I didn't think it wise to come unarmed. And Aggie needs the guns to protect the girls."

"I'm surprised she let you come out at all."

"Agatha isn't my keeper," Philberta said testily. "I had been cooped up inside so long, I needed air." She gazed sadly down at the grave. "That, and I do so miss Esther. Granted, she came into this world dead.

But she was my daughter, Mr. King. Had she lived, she would have been the light of my life. To think! A daughter, after all these years." She appeared about to cry.

Nate quickly changed the subject. "How are Tyne and Anora holding up?"

Jerking her head away from the mound of dirt, Philberta said, "Remarkably well. Children adapt better than adults. So long as they are fed and comfortable, they can endure most anything."

"After you," Nate said, motioning. He let her go by, then snagged the bay's reins and led it around front. To his dismay the door was wide open and no one was standing guard.

"Girls! Agatha!" Philberta hollered.

Aunt Aggie came out, holding a rifle. She smiled warmly at the sight of Nate. "You are the first one back. How did your search go?"

"I will wait and say when the others are here."

Tyne and Anora emerged, Tyne squealing in delight and dashing up to give Nate a warm hug.

"I was worried about you, Mr. King. I don't want you to disappear like my Uncle Sully."

The image of Sullivan's ravaged face floated before Nate, and his stomach churned. "I intend to be on this earth a good long while yet, young one. I have a family of my own I very much want to see again."

Anora said, "I hope Mother and Father are all right."

"And Fitch and Harper," Aunt Aggie reminded her. "Don't forget your brothers." To Nate she said, "Are you staying, or are you going out again? I can fix a meal if you are hungry."

After the horror of the cave, Nate had no appetite.

"A cup of coffee would be nice. Then I have more searching to do."

They all went in and Nate made sure to shut the door after them. "You shouldn't leave this open like you did. The things that killed Sully could sneak right in."

"I left it open in case Philberta needed us and called out for help," Aunt Aggie explained. "What do you mean by 'things'? And how do you know Sullivan is dead if we haven't found his body yet?"

Nate noticed that Philberta had given him a sharp glance. "We don't know what is behind all this," he said, angry at his lapse. "But we can't be too careful." He bobbed his head toward the girls to stress his point.

"I would die before I would let harm come to them," Agatha said. "But your point is well taken. Philberta will just have to stay inside with the rest of us from now on."

"Honestly," was Philberta's response, and she turned away.

Nate placed his Hawken on the table and sank onto a bench. Anora brought a cup of steaming coffee and bowed slightly as a maid might do as she set the cup and a saucer down.

"For you, kind sir."

Nate grinned. "I thank you, gentle lady."

Giggling, Anora scooted over to Tyne, who was poking a stick at the flames in the fireplace.

"The girls are bored, I am afraid," Aunt Aggie said. "They don't think it fair that their brothers got to go out and they didn't."

"They're safer here."

Aggie pulled out the chair across from him. "I wholeheartedly agree. I am only saying."

Philberta joined them, remarking, "This is rough on all of us. On me, most of all. I'm the one who lost a husband and a daughter."

"Don't forget your three sons," Nate said.

"Them too, of course." Philberta placed the knife in front of her, the hilt close to her hand.

Aunt Aggie sighed in sympathy. "Frankly, my dear, I don't know how you held up so long. The terror of being in this place alone would be more than I could bear."

"Oh, pshaw," Philberta said. "You are stronger than you let on. I've always thought you were hardier than Erleen could ever be."

"She is no weakling," Agatha said in defense of her sister.

"Perhaps," Philberta said. "But I can't help think that if it were her husband and sons, she would be in hysterics by now."

"You never did like her much."

"And she has never liked me. I overheard her tell Peter once that as a sister-in-law I leave a lot to be desired."

"Ladies," Nate interrupted, "this isn't the time or place for family squabbles. We are all in this together."

"True," Aggie said.

Philberta shrugged. "No one asked you to come. Not that I'm ungrateful. But you would be smart to leave while you can."

"That's the thanks we get for caring?" Aunt Aggie bristled. "For putting our lives at risk to save yours?"

"You have my undying gratitude. But I don't want to lose all of you, too. And I mean that sincerely."

Nate sipped his coffee and felt it burn a path down

his throat. "Have you seen any sign of Indians the whole time you were here?"

The question gave Philberta a start, but she recovered quickly. "No. No Indians at all. Why do you ask?"

"The Utes are to the southeast, the Nez Perce to the north. The Shoshones live northeast of your valley, other tribes to the west. A hunting party might have happened by and paid you a visit."

"If any Indians knew we were here, they never showed themselves. And I am glad they didn't. I don't like Indians, Mr. King. They are despicable and mean. But what else can we expect from people who live like animals?"

"Philberta," Aggie said softly.

"What?"

"My wife is Shoshone," Nate said. "Maybe you didn't know that."

"No, I didn't," Philberta said. "But it wouldn't change my opinion. Perhaps she is the sweetest woman in the world, but she is still a heathen, is she not? She doesn't believe in God Almighty."

"Since when did you become so religious?" Agatha asked.

"I am speaking in general."

Nate held his resentment in check. "Her people call God the Great Mystery or the Great Medicine. Many are as religious as you can ever hope to be."

"Belief in a false god isn't religion. Why haven't you converted her? Don't you care that she will burn in hell?"

"Philberta!" Aggie said severely.

"I would be remiss not to bring it up. If he loves this Shoshone, he should want her to change her heathen ways."

Nate's coffee had lost its savor. He set down his cup, picked up his rifle, and stood. "I should be going. Expect me back by sunset."

"Finish your coffee, at least," Agatha urged.

"Yes, please do," Philberta said. "I am sorry if my strong talk upset you. But it was for your own good. And for your Shoshone's."

"Her name is Winona."

"A pretty name. But I could never marry an Indian, Mr. King. As for loving one, well, to each their own. I would as soon marry a bear as some greasy buck who spends his days lifting white scalps and his nights scratching himself."

"Philberta!"

Nate headed for the door. He decided he didn't like Philberta Woodrow. He didn't like her at all. "I'll go check on the others."

"Be careful, Mr. King," Tyne said.

Aunt Aggie followed him outside. "Pay no attention to Philberta. She has always been that way."

"I've met her kind before," Nate said. "The ones who think the only good Indian is a dead Indian."

"There is hate on both sides. It's deplorable, but what can we do? Too much blood has been shed. I'm not a bigot like Philberta, but I sometimes think we won't have true peace until all the Indians are on reservations."

"I hope it never comes to that." Nate climbed on the bay and gripped the reins.

"What would you do if war ever broke out between the Shoshones and the whites?" Aunt Aggie asked.

"It never will. The Shoshones are the friendliest tribe on the frontier."

"But if it did. Whose side would you be on?"

"My own. I would do what I thought best for everyone."

Aunt Aggie smiled. "You've chosen a hard path, Nate King."

"I've followed my heart. And I have no complaints, Agatha. My wife is as fine a woman as ever lived. My children try my patience at times, but they are blood of my blood, and I will stand by all three of them, come whatever may."

"I envy them."

"Remember to keep the door closed." Nate wheeled the bay and crossed the clearing to the stream. Fitch and Harper were supposed to be on the other side, scouring their half of the valley. It wasn't long before he found their tracks, and within the hour he spotted the brothers near the cliffs. Unlike the other side of the valley, here there were no bones and no maggot-infested remains.

"Mr. King!" Fitch said as Nate rode up.

"Find anything?"

Both boys shook their heads, their weariness apparent.

"We've looked and looked and haven't come across any sign of Uncle Sully or our cousins," Harper said.

"We're afraid we'll never see them again," Fitch said. "I liked our cousins, too. Norton was the same age as me."

"Don't stay at it too much longer," Nate warned. "Be at the cabin before dark."

"We'll try. But we want to cover this whole side of the valley today, if we can."

"Do as I say," Nate directed. He felt guilty not telling them about what he found. They were old enough to handle it. "Can the two of you keep a secret for the time being?"

"Hope to die if we don't," Fitch said.

"I'm serious. It would upset your sisters. I intended to tell your mother and father first and let them tell the rest of you, but you should know." Nate paused. "I found your Uncle Sully. Or what's left of him. He was killed just like that elk and the Blackfoot."

The brothers looked at one another.

"You did?" Harper exclaimed. "He was? But what killed them, Mr. King? What kind of animal tore that elk apart? And gouged out that redskin's eye like that?"

Nate hesitated. He could be wrong. "It might not have been an animal," was as far as he was willing to commit himself.

"What then? Hostiles? We haven't sign of any."

"I think that whatever"—Nate caught himself—"or whoever killed your uncle is still here. I think they are biding their time and will strike when our guard is down." He gazed at the still-bright sky. "It could be they are waiting for the sun to set. I suspect they like the dark more than the day."

"Who are these 'they' you keep talking about?" Fitch asked.

"What tribe do they belong to?" From Harper.

"I never said they were Indians."

"Who else, then? Are you saying they are white men? A band of cutthroats and killers?"

"They might be white, yes. The important thing is that they will kill you if they get their hands on you, so whatever you do, don't give them the chance."

"We aren't infants."

"Neither are they."

On that note, Nate left. He recrossed the stream, passing close to the cabin to make sure the front door was closed. It took a while to find Peter's and Erleen's tracks. They had gone toward the open end of the valley. He figured they were on their way back by now and he would meet them halfway. But he was almost to the end of the valley himself when he heard a strange sort of *thuk-thuk-thuk*, as if someone were striking the ground. A dozen yards further, and he came on a small clearing. In the center, digging with a branch, was Peter. Over to the left stood Erleen, holding the reins to their horses. Neither noticed him, and he couldn't help but think how easy it would be to kill them. Drawing rein, he cleared his throat.

"Nate!" Erleen hurried over. "I am so glad to see you! You won't believe what we found."

Peter had stopped digging and was mopping his brow with a sleeve. "Who, not what, my dear." He motioned at a blanket draped over a prone form.

"See for yourself," Erleen urged. "But be warned. You need a strong stomach. I am afraid mine wasn't strong enough."

Nate dismounted. "Where did you find him?"

"You've guessed, then?" Peter motioned again. "We found him right where he is. It appears he was dragged here from higher up."

The body of Edwin Ryker had been literally ripped to pieces.

"What did that to him?" Erleen anxiously asked. "What in God's name are we up against?"

Before Nate could reply, from far down the valley, from the vicinity of the cabin, there came a scream of mortal terror.

The Gathering Fear

Fear raced through Nate King's veins as he galloped headlong along the trail. To him, the screamer had sounded like Tyne. But it could just as well have been Anora or one of the women.

Nate was worried they had opened the front door and left it open. He imagined the lurkers in the woods creeping across the clearing and bursting inside before the women had a chance to arm themselves. It would all be over in minutes. Aggie, Tyne, Anora, Philberta, they would all end up like Sullivan and Ryker.

"Please God, no," Nate breathed. The bay was going as fast as it could, but it wasn't fast enough to suit Nate. In his anxiety he lashed the reins and jabbed his heels, trying to get an extra spurt of speed out of the animal.

Somewhere behind him were Peter and Erleen. Nate hadn't waited for them to mount. Nor was he about to slow and wait for them now. He had warned them that something like this might happen, but they had refused to listen. Now he prayed their pigheadedness didn't cost the girls their lives.

Nate approached the last bend before the clearing. He was so intent on the trail ahead that he almost missed movement in the forest to his left. He glanced over and saw a pale figure dart behind a thicket. It moved so quickly that he could not note much detail. But it was on two legs, that much was certain. Adding proof his hunch was right. He almost gave chase. Only the thought that the girls and Aggie might need him kept him flying to their aid.

The cabin door *was* open. Wide open, with no sign of life inside or out. Nate opened his mouth to shout, but his vocal cords were half paralyzed by fear.

A shadow moved across the doorway.

Nate vaulted from the saddle while the bay was still in motion. In his haste he stumbled and almost fell. Then he was running toward the door with the Hawken ready, and forced a cry from his throat. "Aggie! Tyne! Anora! Are you in here?"

Philberta filled the doorway.

In reflex, Nate sprang back and came within a whisker of squeezing the trigger. "Are you trying to be shot?"

"The girls are fine," Philberta said calmly. "They are in here with me. But Aggie went after it."

"After what?"

"Tyne saw something at the window. It was looking in at us. A monster, she called it. Before I could stop her, Aggie ran out. She shouted something about seeing it. When I got to the door she was almost to the woods."

"Where?"

Philberta pointed near a spot near where Nate had glimpsed the pale figure. Stay inside!" Whirling, he sprinted for the trees. He heard horses coming up the trail, but he didn't stop. Philberta could explain to Peter and Erleen.

Nate plunged into the vegetation. "Aggie? Where

are you?" Shouting when an enemy was near was foolhardy but Nate had to find her before the creatures got hold of her. The spectral slayers wouldn't spare her because she was female. Any shred of compassion they possessed had long been extinguished.

Nate came to the thicket and dashed around it, but the pale figure was gone. Nor was Agatha anywhere to be seen. He shouted her name several times while glancing anxiously about. She had to have heard him; she couldn't have gotten that far.

Frantic with worry, Nate skirted a blue spruce and wound through a stand of pines. Suddenly someone was in front of him. He tried to stop but couldn't. Down they crashed, their limbs entangled, Nate shifting so his shoulder bore the brunt for both of them. Pain spiked his arm and he almost lost his grip on his rifle. "You could have given a yell."

Aunt Aggie grunted as she sat up. "I was chasing someone, and I didn't want them to know where I was."

"You should have stayed at the cabin."

"Why? Because I'm female? You would have given chase."

Nate slowly rose and gave her a hand standing. The woods around them were still, but that could be deceiving. "You say that you saw someone? What did they look like?"

"I only saw them for a split second. No doubt you will think I am insane but it was an Indian. A *white* Indian."

"You're right," Nate said.

"You've seen the white Indian yourself?"

Nate grinned. "No, you're right that you are insane. Where did this white Indian get to?"

"I couldn't keep up. I never saw anyone so fast. And the way he ran, hunched over, as if he was a hunchback. I wish I could have seen his face."

"No, you don't." Nate took her elbow and started her back. "What makes you think it was an Indian?"

"The man was practically naked. You don't see white people running around without their clothes on."

"You too?"

"Pardon?" she asked.

"There was only the one?"

"That I saw. I thought if I could shoot him, we could get to the bottom of the mystery. But I never had a clear shot."

"You were lucky."

"Don't you mean he was? I would have shot him and not thought twice about it. He is to blame for the disappearances. I am sure of it."

At last they were in agreement. "So am I. But it's not what you think. It's not what you think at all."

"Then you have some explaining to do, Nate King."

"Soon."

Shouts from the clearing spurred them along. Peter and Erleen had arrived and the girls had come out of the cabin. Philberta stood by the door fingering her knife.

"There you are, Aggie!" Erleen exclaimed. "I was worried to death. Don't you know better than to go chasing savages into the woods? Thank God you weren't hurt."

Agatha whispered to Nate, "She was worried about you, too."

"Sure she was."

Everyone except Nate started to talk at once. Peter

held up a hand, silencing them, and suggested they go inside where it was safe.

"I'll tend to the horses," Nate offered. No one seemed to hear him. Taking the reins to all three animals, he was almost to the corner when he acquired a shadow.

"I'll go with you," Philberta offered.

"I can manage."

"I don't mind." Philberta smiled. "You need someone to watch your back while you strip the saddles."

Nate never expected her to be so considerate. She gave the impression he wasn't high on her list of favorite people.

"I also wanted to talk. I have an idea how we can catch whoever is behind all this."

"I am all ears."

"Bait," Philberta said. "Someone should sit out in the open and lure the heathens in for the rest to shoot."

"Do you have someone in mind?" Nate was willing to bet she wanted him to do it.

"Me."

"You're serious?"

"Never more so. It's a good plan. I'll take some clothes to the stream and wash them. The rest of you can wait in the trees. When the Indians jump me, you can pick them off."

"You'll be in great danger," Nate pointed out.

"Those savages killed my husband and my three sons. I relish the chance to pay them back."

Nate looked at her. She wore a bitter expression, and there was no denying the sincerity in her tone. "We'll talk it over with the others. If they agree, then we'll try it."

"Oh, I'm sure they'll agree," Philberta predicted. "Peter wants revenge on the slayers of his brother."

Nate opened the corral gate and led the horses in. Philberta stood guard, humming. That bothered him. He couldn't say exactly why, other than she was much too cheerful for someone who had lost her family. Should he ever lose his, he would be devastated for years.

The woods stayed quiet. Nate gave the forest a last scrutiny before going in. He had the feeling that unseen eyes were on him again. Closing the door, he barred it.

"Don't put that bar on," Erleen said. "Our boys aren't back yet."

Only then did Nate realize Fitch and Harper weren't there. "They should have heard the scream."

"That was me," Tyne said. "I'm sorry."

"Never apologize for being afraid," Erleen said, giving her a hug. "Fear is natural. I have been scared many times in my life. Why, once I was in the root cellar and a black widow got on my sleeve and I screamed fit to bust my eardrums."

Nate smiled. For all her shrill moments, Erleen tried her best to be a good mother.

"Fitch and Harper will be here soon," Peter declared. "We might as well sit tight."

Nate agreed. But it was plain Peter didn't like waiting, and Nate couldn't blame him. He wouldn't like it, either, not if Zach was out there somewhere, in a valley that harbored—what, exactly? If his hunch was right, what were they? He thought of the book by Mary Shelley, *Frankenstein, or the Modern Prometheus*. Monsters. That was what they were. He was tempted to say something to the others but he held off, on the remote chance he was wrong.

Erleen made coffee for the adults and tea for the children. Peter sat at the table, drumming his fingers. Philberta rocked in the rocking chair, softly humming.

Nate stayed at the window, careful not to show himself. He hoped one of the things would venture into the open so he could get a good look—and a clear shot. But they were too shrewd for that. Even in their state.

Aunt Aggie came over and leaned against the wall. "I will spell you if you want."

"I'm fine."

"It has been almost an hour and no sign of Fitch and Harper. Peter is worried sick but trying not to show it. They should have been here by now, shouldn't they?"

Nate nodded.

"Maybe we're mistaken. Maybe they didn't hear Tyne." Aunt Aggie bit her lower lip. "No. I don't really believe that. I'm trying to convince myself there must be some reason besides the obvious." She clasped her arms to her bosom and trembled. "Lord, no. Not them, too."

"Don't give up hope. They could still be alive."

"You don't believe that. But it is kind of you to say so. You are a kind man, Nate. Is that your given name?"

"Nathaniel."

"I thought so. Isn't it interesting how we always come up with shorter ones? Aggie for Agatha. Nate for Nathaniel. Bob for Robert and Jim for James. As if our given names aren't good enough." Aggie glanced at the table. "You would think we would call Peter Pete but all we ever call him is Peter."

"You bring up the darnedest things."

Agatha looked at him, and then at the others, and lowered her voice to a whisper. "Can I ask you a question?"

"Anything."

"That dead Blackfoot got me to thinking. We're not up against Indians, are we?"

"No."

"Someone else is killing everyone."

"More or less."

"I confess to being confused. And extremely thankful you are here. Left on our own, I'm afraid none of us would survive."

They still might not, but Nate kept quiet.

Agatha tried another tack. "What did you find today when you were out searching?"

"Why do you ask?"

"I flatter myself that I am sensitive to moods and feelings. You were troubled when you came back. Oh, you tried to act natural and pulled the wool over everyone's eyes, except mine. So tell me, Nathaniel. What upset you so much you have seen fit to keep it from the rest of us, presumably for our own good?"

Before Nate could answer, Peter stood and announced, "It's been too long. I am going after my sons."

"It's best if you stay here," Nate said.

"You're a father. Don't tell me you don't understand."

Peter made for the door, and Nate took a step to stop him. But Erleen reached Peter first and planted herself in front of him, her hands on his chest.

"I agree with Mr. King. We should continue to wait."

"How can you say that? They are your boys, too.

Something has happened or they would have been here by now."

Erleen's eyes moistened. "Please, Peter. I couldn't endure it if I lost you."

Peter was disposed to argue, but just then Aunt Aggie called out, "Over here, quick! Something is coming!"

Nate swept a curtain aside as everyone rushed over. The undergrowth across the clearing crashed and crackled to what sounded like a buffalo stampede. But it was a horse. In a flurry of pounding hooves, the animal burst from the forest.

And Tyne screamed again.

Revelations

She had good cause.

The horse was a roan. Harper's roan. It was lathered with sweat and caked with blood. The blood came from a jagged hole in its throat. Another hole, low down on its side, oozed more blood and other fluids. It came to a stop, then staggered toward the cabin, its head hung in exhaustion.

"What did that?" Anora gasped.

"Look at all the bite marks," Aunt Aggie said.

Nate had seen them, all over the roan's legs and belly. Not deep, but deep enough that hair and flesh had been ripped off.

"Was it a mountain lion, do you think?" Erleen asked. "Or could it have been wolves?"

Philberta laughed.

"Neither," Nate said. No animal ever made those wounds.

"It's not the horse that concerns me now," Peter said. "It's our sons. Where *are* they?"

"Little Tommy Tucker sings for his supper," Philberta said.

Everyone looked at her.

Agatha sniffed as if she smelled a foul odor. "You

and those silly rhymes. That was most unseemly, especially with the girls here."

"It's all right, Aunt Aggie," Anora said.

"No, it's not, my dear. Adults must have a sense of decorum. To joke about that poor animal at a time like this is most immature."

Philberta smiled. "Mud in a cake. I saw. I saw."

"Do that one more time and I will slap you."

Erleen asked, "What has gotten into you, Philberta? Granted, you have been through a terrible time, but that's no excuse for your behavior."

"I'm sorry."

To Nate, Philberta didn't sound sorry at all. He made up his mind to keep a close eye on her. At the moment, though, he had the roan to think of. Too weak to stand, it was down on its front knees.

"That poor thing will die soon," Erleen remarked.

"It must be in a lot of pain," Tyne said.

Nate was thinking the same thing. Raising the Hawken to his shoulder, he fixed a bead between the roan's eyes, and told the girls to look away. Someone said something, but he didn't hear for the boom of the rifle. Bone and brains exploded, and the roan keeled onto its side.

"That was awful!" Erleen cried.

"No, it wasn't, dear," Peter said. "The poor animal was suffering. Mr. King put it out of its misery, is all."

Philberta tittered merrily. "Bat, bat, come under my hat and I'll give you a slice of bacon."

The *smack* of Agatha's palm on Philberta's cheek was like the crack of a whip. Anora gasped. Tyne put a hand to her throat. But all Philberta did was take a step back, and smile.

"You really oughtn't. That wasn't very nice."

"I warned you," Aunt Aggie said.

"No more of that." Erleen took Philberta's hand. "Are you all right? It must have stung something awful."

"Three little kittens lost their mittens and they began to cry."

Nate saw the truth begin to dawn on them, saw their shock, their uncertainty. Not a word was spoken as Philberta calmly walked to the rocking chair, picked up her long needles, and resumed her knitting.

"What has gotten into that woman?" Erleen asked of no one in particular.

"Her head was clear for a while, but now it's clouded again," Nate said. "She isn't aware of what she is saying or doing."

"What makes you say that?" Aunt Aggie asked. "What do you know that the rest of us don't?"

"All I have is a hunch," Nate admitted. "But maybe it's time we found out if I'm right." He went to the rocking chair. Philberta continued to knit, and hum. "Do you mind if I ask you a few questions?"

"Catch me if you can, but you can't get me. I'm the Gingerbread Man, is what I am."

"Oh God." Erleen placed her right hand on Anora's shoulder and her left hand on Tyne's. "Maybe my girls shouldn't hear this."

"Let them stay," Peter said.

Nate squatted, his rifle across his knees. "You've been keeping things from us, haven't you, Philberta?"

The *click-click-click* of her needles quickened.

"Don't be afraid to tell us. We only want to help."

"Afraid?" Philberta giggled. "What do I have to be afraid of? I am the little old lady who lived in the shoe."

"What is she talking about?" Erleen asked.

"Those infernal rhymes," Aunt Aggie said.

"Rock-a-bye baby, thy cradle is green." Philberta stopped and looked at Nate. "My baby died, you know."

"Yes. I saw you at her grave, remember?"

"A girl. At long last a girl. And she came out so cold and still. I wanted to cry but I laughed. Can you imagine? I laughed and laughed."

"I am sorry," Nate said.

"I think that's when I knew it had me too."

Erleen interrupted. "What had you? Make sense, will you?"

"Hush, dear," Peter said. "Let Mr. King handle this."

"But—"

"Hush."

Nate was staring at Philberta's eyes, at her dilated pupils. "You told us that when you first settled here, everything was fine for a while. There were a lot of elk and deer for the supper pot. But the game grew scarce and there wasn't as much to eat. Isn't that what you said?" For a few moments he thought she wouldn't answer.

"Yes."

"But that's not the truth, is it?"

Erleen interrupted again. "Are you saying she lied to us? Why on earth would she do that?"

"Consarn it all, Erleen."

"Be quiet, Peter. I am so confused I could scream. What is Mr. King implying?"

Nate didn't take his eyes from Philberta, and her needles. The tips were spattered with dots no one else had noticed. Red dots. "I'm saying the game in this valley wasn't wiped out by hunting."

"Then how?"

"They killed everything they could catch, didn't they?" Nate said to Philberta. "And they are still at it."

"Everything, yes. Rabbits and squirrels and snakes and birds. Deer and elk. Small or big, it makes no difference. They can't help themselves."

"Do you know why?'

"He thought he knew but he was wrong."

"When your family settled here, you ate whatever you thought was safe. Just like you did back in Pennsylvania."

"Sully watched the animals. He always watched the animals. He saw the squirrels eat pine cones so we ate some. I never liked them. They were too hard. We had to break them open, and there wasn't much to them when we did."

"What else?"

"Birds' eggs."

"What else? There has to have been more."

"There were mushrooms."

"I thought so."

"Sully picked several kinds. One was white and tasted like chicken. I liked that one a lot. Another looked like a prune or a fig. Eating it made me hot and prickly."

"Surely my brother knew that some mushrooms are poisonous?" Peter said, aghast.

"Give him more credit," Philberta said. "None of us died. Not from the mushrooms, or from the thorn apples. Everyone says they are bad, but Sully saw birds picking at them and brought some for me to cook. I chopped them up and mixed them with the mushrooms."

"Both at the same time?" Nate was appalled. It

was worse than he thought. Far worse. And it explained everything.

"What's wrong?" Erleen asked. "Why do you look as if she just kicked you?"

"Some mushrooms make us sick but don't kill us. Some do strange things to our minds. They put our heads in a whirl, as the Shoshones like to say." Nate paused. "In other words, they drive us mad."

"Oh, no!"

"Then there are the thorn apples. Maybe you've heard of them under another name. Jimsonweed. It can be used as a poultice for sore joints. But only in moderation. If taken internally, it twists our minds and our bodies. Our temperature climbs to over a hundred. We become irrational." Nate looked up. "There is an old saying about jimsonweed."

"Hot as a fire and mad as a wet hen," Aunt Aggie said.

"That's the one."

Erleen shook her head in bewilderment. "So what you are saying is that the whole family ate the mushrooms and the thorn apples and went stark, raving mad? That it drove them to kill every living thing in the valley?"

"Ask your sister-in-law."

Philberta was knitting once again, the *click-click-click* of her needles a counterpoint to the silence that had fallen. All of them were staring at her in mixed horror and sympathy.

"Does this mean Sully is still alive?" Peter asked. "That he is out there somewhere prowling around like some wild beast?"

"Sully is dead," Nate said. "I saw his body with my own eyes."

"Then who has been doing all the killing? Sully's boys? Norton, Liford and Blayne?"

"They have done a lot." Nate watched the knitting needles. "But I doubt they have done all of it."

"Who else?" Aunt Aggie said.

"Whoever killed Sully poked out his eyes. That Blackfoot had an eye missing too, remember? Not clawed out or dug out. There weren't any scratch marks. The eyes were *poked* out," Nate stressed. He was tempting death, but it had to be done. He had to know—they all had to know—beyond any shred of doubt. "It would take something long and thin to do that." He pointed at the knitting needles. "It would take them."

Philberta shrieked and came out of the rocking chair in a lightning-quick lunge. Even though Nate was expecting it, even though he was balanced on the balls of his feet, he nearly lost one of his own eyes. A needle lanced out, but she wasn't quite fast enough. He felt stinging pain as the tip dug into his temple. She speared at his other eye and he threw himself backward.

Snarling and snapping her teeth, Philberta swung at the others. Aunt Aggie grabbed Tyne and skipped out of reach. Anora, seeking to do the same, tripped and fell. Peter sprang to help her. Erleen was rooted in shock, her mouth agape. Philberta stabbed her in the neck.

"Erleen!" Peter cried.

Wheeling, Philberta bounded for the front door. Nate grabbed at her but missed. Unlimbering a flint-lock, he thumbed back the hammer.

"Aunt Philberta!" Tyne wailed.

Nate didn't shoot. He had her dead to rights. All he had to do was stroke the trigger, and he didn't.

The next instant Philberta threw the bar down and flung the door wide. She glanced back, her face a contorted mask of insanity, an unholy glow in her demented eyes. "Hickory, dickory, dock, the mouse ran up the clock!" she screeched, and was gone.

Nate mentally cursed himself for a fool.

Erleen had a hand to her neck. She tottered as blood seeped between her fingers. "Peter?" she bleated in fright as her knees started to buckle.

Nate went to catch her, but Peter got there in time. He gently carried her to the blankets and carefully laid her down. Aggie and the girls clustered around them.

Not Nate. He ran to the front door in time to catch sight of Philberta as she vanished into the undergrowth. A high, keening laugh wafted on the wind, the sound of lunacy run rampant.

Nate almost went after her. But the family needed him. And he wasn't sure but that Philberta would lead him into a trap. Her insane sons were out there, and if they could catch him as they had caught Ryker—Nate closed and barred the door.

Tyne and Anora were crying. Aunt Aggie was trying to comfort them. Peter was bent over Erleen, his handkerchief to her neck.

"How bad is she?" Nate asked.

"The needle missed her jugular. She'll live, but she needs bandaging." Peter looked over his shoulder. "Do you think my sons are—" He stopped, unable to say it.

Nate could give them false hope, but what purpose would it serve? "They would have shown up by now if they were alive."

"We must hunt Philberta and her boys down and put an end to this," Peter declared.

Gesturing at Erleen and the girls, Nate said, "Now would be a bad time to leave them alone."

"What do we do, then? Stay in here and wait for my sister-in-law and my nephews to come to us?"

"Stop thinking of Philberta and her boys as people. They aren't quite human anymore."

"God help us," Aunt Aggie breathed. "Isn't there something we can do to bring them to their senses?"

"Not that I know of," Nate said.

"I refuse to give up hope." Agatha said. "Some shred of humanity must remain."

As if to prove her wrong, from the woods outside rose savage howls and snarls.

Ghouls in the Night

Nate ran to the window and looked out, but the things in the trees were too crafty to show themselves. He stayed there while Peter and Aunt Aggie cut a towel into strips and tended to Erleen. She had not let out a peep. She just lay there staring blankly at the ceiling.

Aggie made the girls sit at the table and sip tea. "It will help calm your nerves," she told them when Anora said she didn't want any. "Drink it whether you want to or not." She walked to the window. "Anything?"

Nate shook his head.

"There are some things I'm not clear on. How long have you known about Philberta and the others?"

"It took me a while to put the pieces together," Nate said. "I suspected the boys when I found their lair. I wasn't sure about Philberta until she tried to stab me."

Aggie peered skyward. "It will be dark in a couple hours. Will they come after us?"

"Your guess is as good as mine."

Sagging against the wall, Agatha tiredly rubbed her brow. "About Sully. Why did they kill him when he was one of them? Or was he sane?"

"He ate what they ate. Whatever the mushrooms and the thorn apples did to their minds, it did to him, too. But you saw Philberta. They have spells where they seem almost normal. Maybe his head cleared and he tried to stop them. Or maybe they just turned on him."

"Poor Sully. He never should have left Pennsylvania. All he wanted was a better life for him and his loved ones."

"The Oregon Trail is littered with the bones of those who wanted a better life," Nate said. "Some died of hunger and thirst. Some were like Sully and ate things they shouldn't, or drank tainted water." He sighed. "It's the difference between a backwoodsman and a frontiersman."

"I am not sure I understand."

"The East has plenty of backwoodsmen. They live off the land, and they live well. And they think that since they can do it there, they can do it out here. But the West isn't the East. Different animals. Different plants. Different weather. A man has to learn to survive all over again. Once he does, he becomes a frontiersman."

More howls rent the air. Aunt Aggie stiffened and gripped a red curtain until her knuckles were white. "Listen to them," she whispered. "I can scarcely believe that came from human throats."

"A clear shot is all I ask."

Aggie closed her eyes and bowed her chin. "Poor Fitch. Poor Harper. I loved those boys as if they were my own."

"You have the girls to think of now. Don't leave their side. I'll be too busy to watch over them."

Straightening, Aggie nodded. "Don't fear on that score. I won't lose anyone else if I can help it."

The next couple hours were nerve-racking. Nate stayed at the window. Peter never left Erleen's side. He held her hand and stroked her cheeks and tried to get her to say something, but all she did was stare at the ceiling. Aunt Aggie brought out the dominoes, but she had to keep reminding the girls when it was their turn and often they placed a two on a six or a four on a one.

No more howls or others sounds broke the stillness of the forest, not until the sun set and a sliver of crescent moon rose above the high cliffs to cast its silvery glow over the dark valley floor.

Aunt Aggie was lighting a candle when the first cry greeted the moon, an inhuman screech torn from human vocal cords. Soon the night pealed with a hellish chorus that echoed and reechoed off the cliffs until it seemed the valley crawled with the things.

Tyne scampered to Aunt Aggie and burst into tears in her arms. Anora placed her hands over her ears.

Peter glared at the window, and scowled. "I'll be damned if I will listen to that all night."

"There isn't much we can do until the sun comes up," Nate said. So long as they stayed indoors, the lunatics couldn't get at them.

"Look at my wife. I think her mind has snapped. She won't answer me. She doesn't move."

"Shock, probably. It might wear off in a while." Nate was no doctor, but it seemed logical.

Another screech set Tyne to bawling louder.

"Listen to that!" Peter spat. "My own nephews and my sister-in-law! But I swear by the Almighty that won't stop me from squeezing the trigger. I will put an end to them if it's the last thing I do."

Nate didn't like how Peter was working himself up. "Your wife comes first. She needs you by her side."

"She doesn't even know I am here." Peter slumped in despair. "Sullivan, Sullivan, how could you bring us to this?"

The abominations in the woods soon fell quiet. Nate was glad, but wary. Philberta and her brood might try to get at them. With the door barred, the only way in was the window. But they could only come through that one at a time, and he would shoot the first head that poked inside.

"It's time for you two young ladies to think about bed," Aunt Aggie announced. Taking Tyne and Anora by the hand, she escorted them to a far corner. They didn't protest.

Fatigue gnawed at Nate, but he shook it off. He must stay alert no matter what.

Peter dozed sitting up. Aggie turned in, but the way she tossed proved sleep was elusive. The girls managed to fall asleep, but they would whimper and groan.

Above them, the moon crept across the patch of sky.

Nate found it harder to keep his eyes open. He took to pacing, with frequent glances out the window. He had been at it for more than an hour when he stepped to the window for yet another look.

Lit by moon glow, the clearing was empty. The woods were a black tangle that hid their secrets. Nate yawned. He glanced back at the others. They were all asleep, even Agatha. The fire had burned low. He turned back to the window, and his blood turned to ice in his veins.

A face was staring back at him. A pale, hideous, sinister face, framed by a filthy shock of black hair and gristle on the chin. The skin was drawn tight over the bones, the lips were thin and bloodless. But it was the eyes that were truly terrible, eyes lit by inner fires that bordered on the demonic. They glared at him with such raw ferocity, it was like gazing into the eyes of a rabid wolf. Only these eyes evinced far more cunning, and wicked intent.

Whether it was Norton, Liford or Blayne, Nate couldn't say. He suspected it was the oldest. With a start, he galvanized to life and grabbed for one of the pistols at his waist. Suddenly a hand shot through the window and gripped him by the throat. The arm was scrawny, the fingers no thicker than pencils, yet they clamped like an iron vise. Nate could feel his neck constrict as the pressure threatened to pulp his flesh. He grabbed the wrist and pried at the fingers, but it was like prying at metal bands.

The face in the window laughed.

Nate punched the arm. He twisted. He tried to fling himself back. But the madman held on, his fingers closing tighter. Nate's throat was pulsing pain and his chest hurt. He needed air. He must break free, or die. He struck the lunatic's elbow, but the hideous face didn't react. *The face.* Drawing back his arm, Nate rammed his fist into its mouth. The thin lips split and an upper tooth broke but the madman went on squeezing as if he hadn't felt a thing.

Nate's lungs were fit to burst. In desperation he tried to rake the lunatic's right eye with his fingernails, but Norton—if that is who it was—pulled back. Nate did scratch the eyebrow, though, deep enough that blood flowed.

Norton snarled, and blinked, and his hold on Nate's throat slackened slightly.

It was the moment Nate needed. With a powerful surge, he broke the stranglehold. In doing so he lost some of his skin. But that was of no consequence. The important thing was to see to it that no one else suffered Sully's and Ryker's fates. Molding his palm to a flintlock, he brought up the pistol.

The madman was gone. One instant he had been there, and the next he wasn't.

Nate leaned out the window. The lunatic was bolting toward the corner of the cabin. Refusing to let him get away, Nate darted to the door and removed the bar. He was outside and to the corner in seconds, but no one was there.

In frustration, Nate pounded the wall. Whoever it had been could now kill again. Wheeling, he stalked toward the door. Belatedly, he realized his mistake in leaving the door open. Worse, he had left his rifle inside. Fatigue was making him careless and carelessness cost lives.

A slight sound overhead caused Nate to glance up. There, perched on the edge of the roof, were the other two, as pale and feral as their brother, their hair a filthy mess, their skin splotched with bloodstains. They were naked from the waist up and their pants were in tatters. Their eyes had the same demonic quality, as if their human intelligence had been replaced by something from the pit. But the explanation was simpler. They were mad, completely mad, their sole craving to kill and kill again. In their deranged states, they couldn't kill enough. They could never spill enough blood. Animal blood or human blood, it was all the same to them.

Even as Nate glanced up, they sprang. They were smaller and lighter, but there were two of them and their combined weight slammed him onto his back on the hard ground even as their teeth sought his throat and their hands clawed at him like talons.

Nate tried to shout a warning to the Woodrows, only to have a hand shoved halfway down his throat. He gagged on the feel of the fingers and the stench.

The other brother, Blayne, abruptly stood, whirled, and bounded into the cabin.

Heaving up, Nate dislodged the one on his chest. He had barely gained his knees when the madman was on him again. Filthy nails dug at his throat while a mouth rimmed with teeth speckled by bits and pieces of rancid meat gaped to bite his face.

Nate lashed out, a punch to the gut that jolted him. He pushed to his feet, but he was only halfway up when the oldest brother, Norton, flew back around the corner and without slowing or breaking stride lowered his shoulder and rammed into him.

As Nate went down, a shriek filled the cabin. It was followed by a bellow from Peter. A pistol cracked.

Good for them! Nate thought. He hoped they killed Blayne. He wanted to help them, but he had problems of his own. The pair on top of him were attempting to pin his arms.

Then Tyne screamed.

Roaring with rage, Nate exploded upward. He hurled one of the maniacs from him and clubbed the other with his fist. Racing inside, he stopped short in stunned horror.

Erleen was on the floor, her jugular bit open, bucking and kicking and blubbering scarlet down her chin. Peter was unconscious a few feet away, one hand clutching the pistol he had fired, the other spouting blood from the stumps of severed fingers. His throat was intact but not his face; half of it had been ripped off. Anora lay curled in the corner, unmoving.

In the other corner cowered Tyne. Protecting her, armed only with a short-bladed knife, was Aunt Aggie. Speckled with gore, her dress torn, she slashed and stabbed at the nimble figure prancing in front of them.

Blayne cackled as he pranced, his blood-wet fingers hooked like claws. Aggie lanced the knife at him, and he snapped his teeth at her wrist.

Nate groped for his other flintlock, but he had lost it. He drew his bowie and his tomahawk instead. A snarl behind him gave him a twinkling's warning, and he spun. The other two were coming through the door. He swung the tomahawk and connected, but with the flat side and not the edge. It knocked— Liford, was it?—into Norton, and both tumbled back out. Nate whirled again.

Norton had seized Aggie's wrist. She was on her knees, her arm bent at a sharp angle. He was trying to make her drop the knife. Her teeth clenched, she refused to let go.

Nate raced to her aid. He made no noise, yet somehow Blayne sensed him. He released Aggie and turned.

Those demonic eyes locked on Nate's. For an instant, Nate slowed. Only an instant, but enough for Blayne to coil and leap aside as Nate arced the tomahawk in a blow intended to split Blayne's skull.

Most foes, human foes, would have closed with Nate while he was off-balance. But Blayne was as far from human as a human could be. Cackling with demented glee, he did the last thing Nate expected; he ran. Nate gave chase, but Blayne was ungodly quick.

At the door, Nate stopped. He refused to make the same mistake twice. He slid the bowie into its sheath and the tomahawk under his belt. Kicking the door shut, he barred it, then reclaimed his rifle.

Aunt Aggie was cradling Tyne, who sobbed in great, racking heaves.

Erleen had stopped thrashing. She was dead. So was Anora. Her neck was broken. Peter was alive, but his pulse was weak. He had lost so much blood it was doubtful he would last much longer.

Nate covered Erleen and Anora with blankets. He eased Woodrow onto his back and was surprised when Peter's eyes blinked open.

"My family?" The question was a weak rasp.

"Agatha and Tyne are alive."

"Oh God." Peter coughed, and swallowed his own blood. "And Blayne? Tell me you killed him."

"They all got away."

Peter coughed some more. "It can't end like this. You know what you have to do."

"Yes," Nate King said. "I know."

Madmen

The sun had risen an hour before, but it would be another hour before it was above the high cliffs. Gloom shrouded the valley.

Nate glided through a false twilight realm of grays and blacks, every sense alert. In addition to his bowie and the tomahawk, he had his rifle and one of his flintlocks. He'd searched for the other one, but it hadn't been anywhere near the cabin. Someone had taken it. He had a fair idea who.

The squawk of a jay broke the stillness. Somehow, it was reassuring.

The madmen and their mother had come close to exterminating every living creature in the valley, but they hadn't killed all of them.

Nate tried not to think of their latest victims. Before starting his hunt, he had wrapped Peter, Erleen and Anora in blankets and carried them out near the corral. He would bury them later. After. If he lived. If he didn't—he tried not to think of that, either. Aunt Aggie and Tyne would be on their own, with over a thousand miles of wilderness between them and civilization. The prospects of their making it back were slim.

He prayed Aggie kept the front door barred, as he

had told her to, and that she didn't untie the curtains. She had the rest of the rifles and pistols, enough to fend off the lunatics should they try to break in.

The smart thing to do was to mount up and get out of there, to leave the valley to crazed Philberta and her insane brood. But Nate was determined to end it, one way or another. He owed it to Peter. He owed it to himself. So here he was, stalking the dappled woodland, pitting his savvy and his skill against *things* with an insatiable appetite for raw flesh. He could still see that hideous face in the window, still feel those terrible fingers squeezing the life from him. He shuddered, then steeled himself.

The junction of the cliffs appeared ahead. Nate couldn't see the cave yet. He was hoping that was where he would find them.

The silence ate at his nerves. It was so unnatural. Even the wind had died. He avoided twigs and dry brush and anything else that might crunch or crackle and give him away.

Off through the trees the black opening yawned.

Nate went another dozen steps, and stopped. He watched the cave opening for signs of movement, but there were none. If they were there, they were in the inky recesses of their lair.

Wedging the Hawken to his shoulder, Nate advanced. He couldn't wait all day for them to appear. He must force the issue. If they weren't there, they could be anywhere. Maybe at the cabin, about to attack Aggie and Tyne. He must find out.

The sickening stench seemed worse than the day before, if that was possible. Nate fought down more bitter bile. He avoided looking at the grisly remains, and at the legion of flies and maggots crawling over the putrid flesh.

Nate stopped again. He was in clear view, and he braced for a howling rush. But nothing happened. The flies and maggots continued to eddy and the reek filled his nose, but nothing else. They weren't there.

Nate turned to hurry back to the cabin. Yet again, he thought he'd made the right decision and it turned out to be a mistake. He should never have left Aggie and Tyne alone.

Overcome by guilt, Nate nearly missed the patter of feet behind him. He whirled just as the youngest of the three leaped. Blayne's eyes were aglow with unholy bloodlust, and his teeth were bared. In midair he howled. And in midair, Nate shot him.

The Hawken's muzzle was inches from the mad youth's chest when it went off. The heavy slug cored Blayne's sternum, and the impact flipped him onto his back. Growling and spurting crimson, he tried to stand but only made it to his hands and knees when his life fled and his limbs gave out.

Nate had no time to congratulate himself. The other two were almost on him. He dropped the rifle and streaked his hands to his waist. But he had not quite drawn his flintlock and knife when Norton and Liford slammed into him. Teeth sought his throat. Fingers gouged and ripped.

Spinning, Nate sent Norton tumbling. Liford clung on; dementia given form and substance, he shrieked and bit at Nate's jugular.

Jerking aside, Nate tugged his pistol loose and slammed it against the madman's temple. Liford sagged but didn't go down. Nate smashed him a second time, and then a third, crushing an ear and splitting a cheek. But Liford still clung on. Jamming the flintlock against Liford's ribs, Nate fired.

The lunatic staggered. He gawked at the hole in his side and let out a screech of rage and pain. Amazingly, he stayed on his feet and flew at Nate again in a frenzy of teeth and nails.

But Nate had the bowie out. He sheared it into Liford's belly, down low, and sliced upward until the steel grated on rib. Liford's insides spilled out and he collapsed in a heap, dead before he sprawled in the dirt.

Two down, Nate thought to himself. He spun, looking for the third, but Norton had disappeared. Nate had a choice to make. Reload, or go after him. Thinking of Aggie and Tyne, Nate stuck the flintlock under his belt, drew his tomahawk, and dashed into the forest. To his right was a pine, to his left a thicket. He ran between them, watching the thicket since it offered better concealment. Above him a bough swayed, and the next instant a hurtling form slammed into his shoulder blades and he was bowled to the earth.

Norton screeched as he scrambled up into a crouch.

Dazed, Nate groped for his knife. He had lost it when he fell. The madman charged, and Nate cleaved the tomahawk at Norton's contorted face. By rights the keen edge should have split it like a melon, but the lunatic's speed was superhuman. Norton sidestepped, shifted, and sprang at Nate again.

Nate swung, and swung again, but it was like trying to imbed the tomahawk in a ghost. Norton dodged and laughed, and danced and laughed. And just when Nate began to think the madman was treating their life-and-death struggle as some sort of game, he swung again, and missed again, and before he could recover his balance, Norton sprang.

Fetid breath fanned Nate's neck as Norton sought to sink his teeth into Nate's throat.

Nate did the only thing he could think of; he smashed his head into Norton's face. Cartilage crunched, and moist drops spattered Nate's brow. Howling, Norton leaped back, shaking his head to clear it.

His arm a blur, Nate sank the tomahawk into the lunatic's head.

Norton stiffened. Arms rigid, his eyelids fluttering, he tottered. His mouth worked, but no sounds came out. Like mud oozing down a rain-soaked slope, he slowly oozed to the ground. The convulsions he broke into were brief. A last strangled gasp was the last sound he ever made, and then the last of the madmen died.

But Nate wasn't done yet. There was still the madwoman to deal with.

Placing his foot on Norton's chest, Nate gripped the tomahawk handle, and wrenched. He wiped the blade clean on the grass, then gathered his weapons and began to reload. He had finished with the Hawken and was about to load the flintlock when a shot cracked in the distance. On its heels, faint but unmistakable, came a scream.

Fear filling his breast, Nate raced for the cabin. He told himself that Agatha wouldn't be foolish enough to open the door or undo the curtains, that she knew better than to put herself and Tyne at grave risk. But then he remembered the other times she hadn't heeded his advice, and he pushed himself to run faster.

Branches tore at his buckskins. A low limb tried to gouge his eye. Nate plowed on, heedless of the cuts and nicks. He had come a long way and it would take much too long to reach the cabin. By the time he got there, whatever had happened would be over.

Still, Nate didn't slow. He ran until his lungs were fit to rupture and his legs throbbed with pain. He ran until he was caked with sweat from his hair to his toes, and on the verge of collapse. And then the cabin and the corral were only a dozen yards away.

Nate almost called out. But that would give him away. Slowing, he crept forward. The horses hadn't been harmed or let loose, thank God. To be stranded afoot in the Rockies, the old trappers liked to say, was a surefire invite to an early grave.

Nate came to the front of the cabin, and froze. From inside came humming. A chill rippled down his spine. He had to will his legs to move.

The front door was closed, the curtains were still tied shut.

Muffled voices caused Nate's heart to leap into his throat. At least one of them was still alive! He darted to the door, hunkered, and put his ear to it.

"—what you intend to do with us? And this time I would be grateful for an answer, if you don't mind."

Nate had rarely heard a sound as sweet as Agatha's angry voice.

Philberta's titter was laced with lunacy. "Here we go round the mulberry bush, the mulberry bush, the mulberry bush. Here we go round the mulberry bush, on a cold and frosty morning."

"If I never hear another nursery rhyme for as long as I live, it will be too soon," Aunt Aggie said.

"Rain, rain, go away, come again another day."

"Damn you, Philberta. Enough is enough. Talk

plain and simple, not your gibberish. What do you intend to do?"

Nate heard Philberta laugh. Judging by the sounds, Agatha was over near the fireplace. Philberta was nearer.

"My, oh my. What a tart tongue you have, dear Aggie. And you always on your high horse about not swearing in front of the children."

"So you can talk normally when you want to?"

"Billy, Billy come along and I will sing a pretty song."

"Why have you tied me in this rocking chair?"

"The better to keep an eye on you, granny," Philberta said, and snickered.

"I demand you cut me loose."

"There was an old owl lived in an oak, wiskey, wasky, weedle. And all the words he ever spoke were fiddle, faddle, feedle."

"Answer me another question," Agatha prompted. "How is it you're not as insane as your sons? You have lucid moments, do you not?"

"Are any of us ever lucid?" was Philberta's response. "As for the why, I suspect it's because they ate more of the thorn apples than I did. I liked the mushrooms better."

Agatha suddenly asked in alarm, "What are you doing there? Take your hands off Tyne."

Dread choked Nate's breath in his throat. He gripped the latch and lightly lifted but the door wouldn't open. The bar was in place.

"Didn't you hear me!" Agatha cried. "It's bad enough you hit her with that horse pistol. She's lucky you didn't split her head open."

"Oh, I wouldn't call it luck. She should come

around soon, and the moment she opens her eyes, I will send her to join her father and mother and sister."

"Damn you, leave her be! Why are you dragging her toward the pantry?"

Nate didn't wait to hear any more. He remembered what was in the pantry. Rising, he went to throw his shoulder against the door, but then he had a better idea. He darted to the window and compared its width to the width of his shoulders. He could make it. Taking half a dozen quick steps back, he set the Hawken down, lowered his head, and hurtled at the red curtains.

Inside the cabin, Tyne screamed.

Throwing his arms out in front of him, Nate dived through the window. The curtains proved no hindrance. They tore free under his weight and wrapped around his head and shoulders. He landed on his side, and rolled. For a few anxious moments he imagined Philberta about to shoot him as he struggled to free himself from the red folds, but when he cast them aside she was in the pantry, one arm around Tyne's waist and the other at the girl's throat, trying to hoist a struggling Tyne up and impale her on the meat hook.

"Nate!" Aunt Aggie cried. Ropes bound her wrists to the arms of the rocking chair and her ankles to the legs. Blood seeped from a bullet wound in her right shoulder.

Philberta saw him. A look of raw hate and crazed ferocity came over her. Suddenly screeching in rage, she lifted Tyne off the floor and turned her so Tyne's back was to the meat hook.

"*No!*" Nate flew toward the pantry.

"Mr. King!" Tyne wailed, kicking and twisting, tears streaming down her face. "She's going to kill me!"

Not if Nate could help it. He was not aware of drawing his bowie but it was in his hand when he reached the pantry door.

Philberta couldn't lift Tyne high enough. Suddenly flinging the girl against the shelves, she reached behind her. When her hand reappeared, she held the two blood-spattered knitting needles. "I've had enough of you!" she shrieked, and was on him in a whirlwind of flying arms and needles.

Parrying with the bowie, Nate gave way. He wanted Philberta out of the pantry and away from Tyne. His ploy worked. Snarling and hissing, Philberta came after him.

Nate retreated faster. He bumped into the table and shifted to dash around to the other side to put the table between him and Philberta. But she was too fast. A needle sliced into his arm. She raised her other arm to stab him in the face. That was when he drove the bowie into her chest, clear to the hilt. Philberta gasped, and threw her head back. The gasp became a gurgle as Nate twisted the blade, severing her heartstrings.

Philberta looked at him and the light of insanity faded from her eyes. Or so Nate thought until she said, "Little Bo-Peep has lost her sheep." And then she was gone.

Nate pulled the bowie out and stepped back. Suddenly Tyne was there, throwing her arms around his legs and crying into his buckskins. "She's gone," Nate said. "It's all right." But it would never be completely all right for either of them, ever again.

Aunt Aggie cleared her throat. "When you two are ready, I am tired of sitting in this chair."

Nate picked up Tyne and carried her over. A few strokes and the deed was done. Aggie took the girl in her arms and held her close, and together they walked out of the cabin into the clear bright light of day.

"When you think of the West, you think of Zane Grey." —*American Cowboy*

ZANE GREY

THE RESTORED, FULL-LENGTH NOVEL, IN PAPERBACK FOR THE FIRST TIME!

The Great Trek

Sterl Hazelton is no stranger to trouble. But the shooting that made him an outlaw was one he didn't do. Though it was his cousin who pulled the trigger, Sterl took the blame, and now he has to leave the country if he wants to stay healthy. Sterl and his loyal friend, Red Krehl, set out for the greatest adventure of their lives, signing on for a cattle drive across the vast northern desert of Australia to the gold fields of the Kimberley Mountains. But it seems no matter where Sterl goes, trouble is bound to follow!

"Grey stands alone in a class untouched by others." —*Tombstone Epitaph*

ISBN 13: 978-0-8439-6062-4

COTTON SMITH

"Cotton Smith is one of the finest of a new breed of writers of the American West."

—Don Coldsmith

Return of the Spirit Rider

In the booming town of Denver, saloon owner Vin Lockhart is known as a savvy businessman with a quick gun. But he will never forget that he was raised an Oglala Sioux. So when Vin's Oglala friends needed help dealing with untruthful, encroaching white men, he swore he would do what he could. His dramatic journey will include encounters with Wild Bill Hickok and Buffalo Bill Cody. But when an ambush leaves him on the brink of death, his only hope is what an old Oglala shaman taught him long ago.

"Cotton Smith is one of the best new authors out there."

—Steven Law, Read West

ISBN 13: 978-0-8439-5854-6

ANDREW J. FENADY

Owen Wister Award-Winning Author of *Big Ike*

No mission is too dangerous as long as the cause—
and the money—are right. Four soldiers of fortune,
along with a beautiful woman, have crossed the
Mexican border to dig up five million dollars in
buried gold. But between the Trespassers and their
treasure lie a merciless comanchero guerilla band,
a tribe of hostile Yaqui Indians and Benito Juarez's
army. It's a journey no one with any sense would
hope to survive, or would even dare to try, except...

The Trespassers

Andrew J. Fenady is a Spur Award finalist and re-
cipient of the prestigious Owen Wister Award for
his lifelong contribution to Western literature, and
the Golden Boot Award, in recognition of his contri-
butions to the Western genre. He has written eleven
novels and numerous screenplays, including the
classic John Wayne film *Chisum*.

ISBN 13: 978-0-8439-6024-2

LOUIS L'AMOUR
TRAILING WEST

The Western stories of Louis L'Amour are loved the world over. His name has become synonymous with the West for millions of readers, as no other author has so brilliantly recreated that thrilling and unique era of American history. Here, collected together in paperback for the first time, are one of L'Amour's greatest novellas and three of his finest stories, all carefully restored to their original magazine publication versions.

The keystone of this collection, the novella *The Trail to Crazy Man*, features the courage and honor that characterize so much of L'Amour's best work. In it, Rafe Caradec heads out to Wyoming, determined to keep his word and protect the daughter of a dead friend from the man who wants to take her ranch— whether she wants his help or not. Each classic tale in this volume represents a doorway to the American West, a time of heroism and adventure, brought to life as only Louis L'Amour could do it!

ISBN 13: 978-0-8439-6067-9

LOREN ZANE GREY

continues in the grand tradition of his father,

Zane Grey,®

with the further adventures of Lassiter—
the rough-riding hero from
RIDERS OF THE PURPLE SAGE
who became one of the
greatest Western legends of all time.

LONE GUN

When Lassiter promises to protect his dead friend's son, he never thinks the young rancher will run into such a passel of trouble. Yet before he knows it, there's an all-out range war led by a pack of hired sharpshooters trying to steal the kid's land—and their lives. They figure that one man can't last long, but they haven't reckoned on...

THE LASSITER LUCK

ISBN 13: 978-0-8439-5815-7

☐ YES!

Sign me up for the Leisure Western Book Club and send
my FREE BOOKS! If I choose to stay in the club, I will pay
only $14.00* each month, a savings of $9.96!

NAME: _____

ADDRESS: _____

TELEPHONE: _____

EMAIL: _____

☐ I want to pay by credit card.

☐ VISA   ☐ MasterCard   ☐ DISCOVER

ACCOUNT #: _____

EXPIRATION DATE: _____

SIGNATURE: _____

Mail this page along with $2.00 shipping and handling to:
Leisure Western Book Club
PO Box 6640
Wayne, PA 19087
Or fax (must include credit card information) to:
610-995-9274

You can also sign up online at **www.dorchesterpub.com**.
*Plus $2.00 for shipping. Offer open to residents of the U.S. and Canada only. Canadian
residents please call 1-800-481-9191 for pricing information.
If under 18, a parent or guardian must sign. Terms, prices and conditions subject to
change. Subscription subject to acceptance. Dorchester Publishing reserves the right to
reject any order or cancel any subscription.